yn'r'enjiy,
Lrel,
Ralerle

Beautifully Broken:

The Life of Danielle Lee

R.D Bush

Beautifully Broken: The Life of Danielle Lee. Copyright © 2020 by R.D Bush.

ISBN: 978-1-7351268-1-4

Printed in the United States of America

First Printing 2021

Dedication

My life and journey wouldn't be possible if it wasn't for Jehovah. He has seen me go through it and he has rescued me many times. Despite the good, the bad and the ugly, He has forgiven me. I am so thankful he loves me.

My children have been my inspiration, my joy and my life.

Thank you, the man I love. You were my inspiration. I want to be your whale (insider) but I want you to find your happy and hopefully its me. I love you.

Lastly, I want to thank everyone for teaching me, loving me, hating me and trying me. Without any of you, this book would have never been possible.

–Ral

Chapter 1

Danielle pulled up to her son's school in her black Range Rover. It had dark, tinted windows with a white leather interior. The vehicle was a gift from her husband, Stefan. He loved to spoil her, but in the beginning of their relationship that wasn't the case. The truck had two TV's in the back, which helped keep the children occupied on long drives. She always dreamed of having a Range Rover and was thankful to Stefan for making her dreams come true.

Mason exited the car and ran toward his friends. Danielle saw a woman with a teenage daughter, a young son and a little girl in a stroller. She could hear the woman yelling at the little boy, who failed to hold on to the stroller as they crossed the street.

Danielle thought back to when that was her. Now, her daughter was twenty-one years old, her son was nine, her identical twin daughters were six, and she was six months pregnant with her and Stefan's first child together. She thought back to when it all started and reflected on all that it took for her to get to where she was today.

"Girl, Michelle took me to Paterson and we were hanging with some of her guy friends that she knows from out there. She brought Renee along, and girl, she was in the bathroom with one of the dudes getting her pussy ate out," Shante said on the other end of the phone line. "Where were you?"

"I had to work my second job at Garden State Plaza and I had a project my professor said I better not hand in late. I'm always leaving class early or not going because I'm too busy spending time with Gus."

Gus was a sexy Colombian guy with long braids down his back, which was one of the main things that attracted Danielle to him. He was three years her senior and she had met him at Rhumba's, a club in the Bronx on E Tremont Avenue. Gus however, lived in Paterson on Twenty-first Avenue. The two had been seeing each other for four months and he took up a lot of her time.

"Were the guys Black or Spanish?" Danielle asked.

Michelle, Shante and Danielle came from religious families and grew up together in the same church. All three of them loved Spanish boys. Danielle always said she would never be involved with a Black guy, and if she did, he couldn't be darker than her.

Danielle was five-three and 124 pounds. She had a round face with chinky-shaped eyes, a pug nose and cocoa brown skin. Danielle was the only one out of the three with an actual shape. Michelle was five-eight and 125 pounds. She had a round face,

2

a wide nose and medium brown skin. Michelle was the more sexually experienced out of the three of them. She was promiscuous and even experimented with the lesbianism at one time but was fully into men now. Shante was five-five, 120 pounds, had dark brown skin, a pointy nose and wore glasses. She was the only one that was still a virgin.

"Yes, they were all *Papi's*. I only thought one was cute. They called him Vargas, and I think he and Michelle had a thing going on."

"Next time, I will definitely hang with y'all. Paterson is like a candy store but instead of candy it is full of fine men. So many choices, you don't know who to pick," Danielle laughed.

A few weeks passed and Danielle got a call from Michelle.

"Hey girl," Michelle said, on the other end of the phone. "Shante has an open crib this weekend. You want to come over and spend the weekend with us?"

"Yeah, of course. What's the plan?"

"Nothing specific. We can go see what's up with my boys in P-Town and see what we can get into."

"Oh, yes. I'm definitely down!" Danielle said with excitement.

The next day, Michelle arrived at Danielle's house in her mom's green, four-door 1998 Mazda 626. Danielle was living in Newark at her paternal grandmother's house because her mom, stepdad and maternal grandmother all moved to North Carolina a few months ago.

The two arrived at Shante's house in Bergenfield, New Jersey. Shante lived in a big white house in a cul-de-sac in a predominantly white neighborhood. Shante's mother had her as a teenager, so her grandmother and her husband, who was an orthopedic doctor, had adopted Shante when she was just a baby.

After ordering pizza and figuring out their plans for the night, they headed over to Paterson and met up with Michelle's friend Diablo at a big park known as Eastside Park.

Diablo was only about four-nine, had a round face, small eyes, and a dimple in his chin. He was fair skinned because he was Irish and Puerto Rican. He was cute but his height was a turn off in Danielle's eyes.

Diablo was in the middle of a smoking cypher and had a blunt in his hand when the girls pulled up.

"What's up, Chelle?" Diablo said.

"Nothing much. My girls and I wanted to get into something, so I wanted to see what you were doing. These are my girls, Shante and Danielle. We have open crib at Shante's if you want to hang out over there."

"Oh, really? Alright. Well let's go by Eastside High and see what a few of my boys are doing. Your boy Vargas is over there too," he chuckled.

Michelle drove Diablo and the girls over to Eastside High, which is famously recognized because of the movie *"Lean on Me."*

When they got to the school, Diablo and Michelle saw Vargas. Vargas had a light tan complexion with shoulder length braids. He was Puerto Rican and stood about five-nine and 180 pounds. He had on some baggy jeans, black hi-top sneakers and a black hoodie. He walked up to the car and spoke to Diablo and Michelle, then looked in the backseat.

"Michelle, who is your friend?" Vargas asked, as he looked at Danielle.

"I am right here. You can just ask me who I am," Danielle answered.

Vargas laughed and looked her in the eyes. "You're cute. What's your name?" as he bit his lip.

"I'm Danielle," she answered. Just then, two more of Vargas's boys, Jose and Mario, walked up to the car. Jose was Puerto Rican, five-six, light skinned and had a facial expression that reminded Danielle of a pit bull. He came off as if he was angry at the world. Mario was Dominican and gangly-framed, topping out at about six feet with a tan complexion and was very attractive. But he was the youngest out of the crew at sixteen years old.

Michelle asked Vargas if they all wanted to chill with her, Shante, Danielle and Diablo back at Shante's house. They all agreed.

When they got to Shante's house, Shante showed everyone around the five-bedroom, four full bathroom house, and made it very clear that no smoking was permitted. The guys decided to hang out in the finished basement where they watched TV and listened to music. The girls were upstairs in the kitchen talking about who they thought was cute. Danielle had her eye on Vargas. He kind of turned her on with their opening conversation. Shante didn't find any of them her type. She was more into white boys. Unbeknownst to Shante and Danielle, Michelle and Vargas already had a sexual encounter, so she stayed quiet.

The girls ended up taking their conversation upstairs to one of the guest rooms. Shortly after, the boys appeared after they finished discussing which girl they wanted and their plan to get pussy.

The guest room the girls were in had two beds. Michelle was sitting on the bed closer to the bedroom door. Shante and Danielle were on the other bed located on the other side of the room. The guys entered the room. Diablo, Mario and Jose all sat next to Michelle, while Vargas sat next to Danielle.

Vargas started to make his move on Danielle, but she came off as not interested even though she did find him cute. Vargas was a player. He was raised on the streets and knew what to do and say to get into a female's panties. Especially a female like Danielle, who didn't come from the streets and was just getting a taste of the outside world.

Vargas had just turned twenty, while Danielle was nineteen and still very inexperienced in life. She was very naïve when it came to guys. Especially a guy like Vargas, whose main objective was to get laid.

Vargas came to New Jersey from Puerto Rico when he was a little kid not knowing a word of English. He lived with his father and two brothers. His father had taken him and his brothers from their mother after he found out that she had gotten pregnant by his brother back in Puerto Rico.

When Vargas was a pre-teen, his father's girlfriend raised him for a few years because his father went to jail for molesting Vargas's young female cousins, which explained his lack of respect for women. He started having sex at the age of twelve and was a father for the first time by the time he turned fifteen and again at the age of seventeen.

While Vargas was trying to kick game to Danielle, they heard Michelle scream.

"GET OFF ME!"

Diablo, Jose and Mario were all trying to feel her up. Michelle didn't mind the attention, but she was jealous of the fact that Vargas was giving his undivided attention to Danielle and not her.

Michelle stormed out the room and went into Shante's bedroom. Danielle and Shante quickly followed.

"What happened?" Shante asked.

"They were all feeling up on me," Michelle replied. "I felt like they were trying to rape me."

Meanwhile, the guys stepped outside in the backyard to smoke a cigarette.

"That bitch was getting wet until she saw you macking it to her friend, Vargas," Diablo said.

"Yo, I don't want her ass. But her friend, I'm definitely smashing," Vargas replied.

When they finished smoking, they headed back upstairs and knocked on Shante's bedroom door.

"Y'all good in there?" Diablo asked, as he knocked on the door.

Danielle asked Michelle, "Are you really okay?"

"I'm fine," she said, with a snarky attitude in her voice.

"We're good. We will be out in a few," Danielle yelled from inside the bedroom.

The guys headed back downstairs. After making sure Michelle was good, Shante headed downstairs to see what the guys were doing. She couldn't afford for them to mess up or steal anything out of her house.

"Where's Danielle?" Vargas asked.

"She is upstairs in the guest room laying down."

Danielle was tired and went to lay down alone in the spare room. She secretly wanted Vargas to come upstairs and keep her company. Meanwhile, Vargas was glad Danielle was alone and exactly where he wanted her to be. He walked into the bedroom and closed the door.

"Whatcha doing alone? Were you up here waiting for me?" he asked with a laugh.

Danielle started to blush.

"I wanted to lay down, and no I wasn't waiting for you, but you can lay next to me if you want."

Vargas knew he was about to get him some.

At first, he laid next to Danielle and they started talking. Then suddenly, he started kissing her neck. Danielle started to feel desire curling low in her belly.

"What are you doing?"

Vargas didn't reply with words. Instead he lifted up her shirt and started to suck on her breast.

"Oh my God," Danielle whispered, as she arched into him.

He went from one breast to the other, sucking on them. Then he started going lower, trailing kisses down her stomach until he got to her pussy. He was a master at pussy eating.

He started to lick around her pussy and kiss her inner thighs. Then he went in for the kill. He licked and sucked on her pussy, twisting his tongue in and around her insides.

Danielle started to feel a rush. Vargas got on top and started grinding on her.

"If you let me stick it in, you could feel amazing."

Danielle was tempted, but she was already fucking Gus.

"Nah, I don't want you to stick in in," Danielle said, with her hands on his chest trying to back him up.

Vargas was disappointed but he knew he had her in the bag. He ate her pussy out so good he knew she would be back for more.

Vargas left the room to join the guys back downstairs. As Danielle laid in bed, her mind kept replaying the feeling Vargas gave her until she finally dozed off to sleep.

Vargas liked Danielle, but he liked her the way he liked all the other girls he was messing with. He was not looking to settle down with anyone. He was living his life. Plus, Danielle lived in Essex County and didn't have a car. It wasn't like he would see her often or at all. What Vargas didn't know was that Danielle was the type that wanted a relationship and eventually a family. Now that she had her eye on him, she was going to try and make something out of what she thought they had. Danielle didn't know anything about the streets or how guys like him were not into settling down and having a relationship. Guys like Vargas came with drama she was not accustomed to.

"Hello, New Jersey Transit, how can I help you?" the woman said over the phone.

"Yes, I would like to know what bus I can take from Newark to Park Avenue in Paterson," Danielle asked.

She hadn't seen Vargas in a week, and kept thinking back to Shante's house when he ate her out. She wanted to see him again. She didn't know where he lived or where he hung out. She was going to walk past the house Michelle dropped him off at, which was near Eastside High, and walk around. Maybe she would run into him, Mario or Jose. She was going to take a chance, hop on the bus and make it her mission to see him.

9

She got off the bus at Paterson Broadway Bus Terminal. From there she walked to Market Street until she reached the fast-food restaurant Checkers and started walking on Park Avenue. She walked past Eastside High where she only saw a few high school kids hanging around outside. Once she got to the bodega next to the school, she turned right and walked past the house Michelle dropped him off at. As she walked past the house, she tried to look up at the porch where she saw some dudes standing around who sounded like they were throwing dice. She crossed the street so she could have a better view of the guys on the porch. After getting a better view, she saw Mario.

Danielle felt her heart throb. She felt like a stalker just popping up in a town she knew little about and going to Vargas's hood, not knowing anyone out there.

She took a deep breath, walked across the street and walked up on the porch.

"Hey Mario. What's up? I was wondering if you have seen Vargas?" Danielle asked, with all the eyes on the porch stopping to stare at her.

"Oh, hey Danielle. Nah, I ain't seen him. Did he know you were coming over here?" Mario asked, making her feel even more stupid for coming out there.

"Nah. I was down the street at my cousin's house and was just walking past," Danielle lied. "When you see him, tell him I was looking for him. Here, take my number and have him call me when you see him."

"No doubt."

Danielle didn't know what came over her. She went all the way to Paterson to pop up on a dude she only met once. She

10

really wanted to get to know Vargas and wanted him to fall in love with her…maybe even start a family.

The next day Vargas called Danielle. The two started communicating weekly, then it turned into daily. Soon Danielle broke things off with Gus. After three weeks, Vargas asked Danielle to be his girlfriend. Dating Vargas was a totally different world for Danielle. He was a runner and a block hugger. He sold bags of dope for eight dollars on the corner of East Nineteenth and Park Avenue for a chubby, white skinned Puerto Rican named Blanco. Being with a drug dealer was never Danielle's goal in life, but it brought excitement. Being that she was gullible and lived in the fantasy world, Vargas knew how to easily manipulate her. Whenever the cops would run down on the block, Vargas would have her hold the drugs. "Baby, the cops won't bother you. You look too boujee for them to ever suspect you of anything illegal," Vargas would tell her. Danielle would never question him. She wanted to be his Bonnie and him, her Clyde. She would often fantasize how they could be successful in the drug game, but Vargas never took her ideas seriously. Danielle felt they were getting closer and closer and thought she was starting to grow serious feelings for him, not realizing he only kept her around because her pussy was so damn good.

After dating for two months, Danielle took the bus to Godwin Avenue, which was the new block Vargas was hustling on in Paterson's fourth ward, a more dangerous part of town. She located him on the side of a house serving a dope fiend.

"Babe, what you doing over here? I'm working," Vargas said when she walked up to him.

11

"I was thinking about you. We live so far apart so I just decided to come see you," Danielle replied with a smile.

"Well, I'm glad you came because I need to talk to you anyway."

"Oh, really. What's up?" Danielle said with excitement.

Vargas took a deep breath. "Well, my baby mom came over here the other day. She wants to get back with me."

"Ohhhh yeah, what did you tell her?" Danielle asked with a smile. *I know he told her he had a girl and wasn't beat to get back with her,* she thought to herself.

"We have a kid together and I told her we can try and work it out. So with that being said, I am going to have to break up with you. You know how it is."

Danielle's heart dropped. She was at a loss. She thought he really cared for her, but now he was breaking up with her.

"I'm sorry. I really do like you, but I got to do what's right for my son."

Danielle wanted to cry but she held her tears back. "I wish you luck and I'll miss you," she said, as Vargas gave her a goodbye hug.

There was nothing else to say. Danielle turned and walked back toward Broadway with her head down and tears rolling down her face.

Meanwhile, Vargas had started messing with a girl that lived on the block. He had to put an end to Danielle just popping up and threatening what he was trying to accomplish with his new boo, Kia. The lie he cooked up quickly about his baby mom was brilliant and Danielle easily fell for it.

Meanwhile, Danielle's grandma was dealing with a cancer diagnosis, but she was getting up and out more, so everything

12

seemed to be improving. One Tuesday morning in June, Danielle got up early to catch the bus so she could be in Englewood by 9 AM for work. Danielle was working at a doctor's office as a receptionist. She had been working there for about a year now, but since starting college, she scaled back to only working part-time, and also worked at Footlocker in the mall part-time as well. The travel time on the bus from Newark to Englewood took her three hours each day. As Danielle was leaving, she waved goodbye to her grandma, who was up getting ready for a doctor's appointment. It was just a regular day until Danielle got home from work that evening.

"Where are you guys going?" Danielle asked, as she saw her brother Bobby and step-granddad getting in the car.

"Grandma went to the doctor today and they kept her. The hospital just called and said that we need to get up there now," Bobby answered.

Danielle hopped in the car with them and they headed to Barnabas Hospital in Livingston, New Jersey.

Not even two minutes after they arrived at the hospital, the light above her grandma's door started flashing, and nurses rushed into the room. A few minutes passed and the doctor came out.

"Sorry. We did all that we could, but she didn't make it," the doctor announced.

Danielle felt as if it was a dream. She just saw her grandma that morning and waved goodbye and knew she would see her later. How can someone go to the doctor and not come back home alive?" *Maybe I stressed her out because I was staying out late,* Danielle started thinking. Danielle's thoughts were all over the place as she tried to process what was going on.

The nurses allowed Danielle to go in the room and say her last goodbyes.

After her step-grandad left out the room from saying his goodbyes, it was Danielle's turn. When she walked in the room and it was a mess. You could tell the doctors and nurses had been in there trying to do everything they could to keep her alive. A tube was still in her grandma's mouth. Danielle stood next to her now deceased grandma, took her hand and started crying. Danielle bent down on her knees and kissed her grandma's hand. She apologized for not listening, for always giving her a hard time, for sneaking Vargas into her house and for not appreciating her. With tears flowing from her eyes Danielle started begging her to get back up. As reality started to set in, that her grandma was gone, more the tears started rolling down her face. Danielle didn't want to leave her grandma, but the nurses came in and told her it was time for her brother to come say his goodbyes because they would have to remove her body from the room soon.

Within a month Danielle had experienced heartbreak and now her grandma was gone. Four days later her grandma was buried, and soon after her step-grandad told her she had to find somewhere else to live.

Danielle's co-worker from the doctor's office found her a room to rent in North Bergen, New Jersey, which was in Hudson County. It was a relief because she didn't know what she would've done. It was like everything was happening back-to-back.

Danielle wanted to stay focused since she was working two jobs. She was about to be twenty years old in August and was making $10.50 per hour at the doctor's office, and $9.00 per hour at her part-time job at the mall. She also made some extra money on the side selling sneakers since she had gotten a connection from her second job. She loved her job at the sneaker store, but didn't get along with one of her coworkers, a girl Danielle went to high school with that was two grades underneath her. Everyone called her Sealy because she looked like Whoopi Goldberg's character in the movie *The Color Purple.*

"Roy, I left my sneakers at my other job, so after the staff meeting can I go get them?" Danielle said to her manager at Footlocker.

"Sure," Roy replied, as he waved her off.

After catching the bus to her other job and returning to the mall, Danielle started folding shirts by the cash register next to Roy.

"Why did she get to leave and come back because she forgot her sneakers? She called out the other day because she said her grandma died, but her grandma died last month I heard," Sealy started saying to Roy.

Danielle couldn't deny she had called out and used the excuse her grandma died even though it was over a month now. *Why was Sealy trying to make problems?* Danielle wondered.

"You can address me, I'm right here," Danielle said.

Sealy was speaking to Roy about her as if she wasn't standing right there.

"I'm talking to Roy, but I'll see you outside after work because I don't like you anyway," Sealy replied.

Danielle put the shirt down that she was folding and walked over to Sealy and punched her in the face and said, "You can see me now!"

Sealy looked as if she was in shock. A lady and her son who were in the store at the time rushed out quickly.

Roy couldn't believe what he just saw. "Danielle, go get your stuff. I'm sending you home."

"She threatened me. Oh man, I hope I'm not fired."

"Just get your belongings. I'll call you later," Roy answered with a sigh.

Danielle headed to the back. She was pissed because she knew she was going to be fired.

As soon as she came out of the back, Sealy was standing in the mall right outside of the store.

"Oh bitch, I'm ready for you now!" Sealy yelled at Danielle.

Danielle threw her bags down and met Sealy out in the mall. Sealy lunged at Danielle but missed. Danielle was able to grab Sealy by her dreads and wrapped them around her arm and put her into a headlock. Sealy was trying to worm her way out of the headlock, but Danielle's grip was strong. Roy had to send two male employees that were in the store to pull Danielle off her. Finally, after separating the two women, Roy told her she was now fired and that if she had just left the store, he could have helped her save her job. But since she continued to fight, he had no choice but to let her go. As soon as he told her that, she turned around and the Paramus Police were right behind her.

They took a statement and told Danielle they would be in touch, because Sealy wanted to press charges against her for assault.

Danielle walked to bus stop crying. She needed and loved that job, but now she got herself fired all because a dumb ass bitch was hating.

That weekend Danielle went to Paterson to release stress by shopping and was hopeful that she would run into Vargas. Soon as she hopped off the Jitney Bus on Main Street, Vargas walked right past her and was shocked to see her. Danielle took that as a sign that they were meant to be. He was walking with his friends as if they were all in a rush.

"Hey D, what's up? I can't really talk right now, but I'll page you later if you're still around."

Danielle just knew she was going to see him later.

After she finished shopping, Vargas still hadn't paged her. It was 5 PM and the stores would close in an hour. She didn't want to go all the way back to Hudson County until she saw Vargas. Danielle did some window shopping and browsed inside some of the stores. After the stores closed, she decided to walk to Market Street and get some food from McDonald's. After sitting there for an hour and still hearing nothing from Vargas, she decided to walk back to Main Street to take the Jitney Bus back home. She was disappointed she wasted the entire evening in Paterson waiting for a beep. After being on the bus for ten minutes, Vargas finally beeped her. She got off the bus immediately and walked to the closest pay phone and called him back.

"Are you still in town?" he asked.

"Yeah, I just walked to the bus stop. I was about to leave," Danielle lied.

"Come through. I'm on Slater Street at my pops house. It's off Main Street, a block away from the jail."

Danielle hopped on another Jitney Bus going back toward Slater and got off.

Vargas was standing outside smoking when Danielle

17

approached. They went inside where his younger brother Carlos, aka Flex, and his cousin Chino were sitting. Chino was half Ecuadorian, on the heavy side and had long black hair that he had in braids. Flex was darker than Vargas, and medium built with a big head. He also had his hair done up in cornrows.

"We are about to leave. I'm going to call a cab to drop us off on Godwin Avenue, where I'm staying."

"Ok, cool." Danielle was super excited to be with Vargas. She missed him and needed to feel loved.

The cab dropped them off at a raggedy white house at the end of Godwin Avenue. Vargas and Danielle went upstairs to the room he rented. Vargas was very neat, so his room was clean and the bed was nicely made. When Danielle went to the bathroom to freshen up, Vargas turned the radio on to Hot 97. He gave her an extra pair of pajama pants he had laying around. They caught up with each other and after talking for about an hour, Danielle went to lay down on the bed. As soon as she laid down Vargas knew exactly what to do. He went to the end of the bed and pulled the pajama pants off her. He dragged her legs down to the end of the bed so that her pussy was in his face when he bent down. He opened her legs and started licking her pussy up and down and lapping his tongue against her clitoris. Danielle started to scream. He continued sucking on her clit and fingering her at the same time. He continued for another five minutes and Danielle wanted to explode. She was ready for his dick.

"Slide it in now," she whispered loud enough for him to hear. Vargas took his shirt off and got on top of her. He started sucking on her breast and wrapped his mouth around her nipple sucking it; first the left one then the right one. Danielle was getting more and more turned on. Vargas could feel her excitement building and finally slid his dick in. Danielle started to moan as R&B singer Aaliyah's song, "Rock the Boat," started playing on the radio. Vargas started grinding his dick inside of her and her body was following the motion. She trembled and her pussy tightened around his dick. "Damn baby, this pussy is good," he whispered in her ear.

Danielle let out a throaty moan as she came.

"You came, babe?"

"Yeah, ohhhhhhh that dick felt good," she said, as she continued to rhythmically tighten her pussy around his dick. She was ready for another round. "I want you to come," she answered.

"I came already," Vargas said, as rolled off her and lit a Newport 100.

Danielle got up and went to the bathroom to freshen up. The two laid down and cuddled until they fell asleep. Danielle stayed with Vargas for two days. She was happy she had her man back.

Chapter 2

Danielle and Vargas communicated daily and spent a few days a week together. A month and a half had passed since they rekindled their relationship and Danielle realized her period was late.

She made a doctor's appointment, and it was confirmed that she was in fact pregnant.

Danielle called her good friend Lisa on her lunch break.

"Lisa, you busy?"

"No, girl, just was arguing with Tyrone's stupid ass. I'm tired of his bum ass laying up in my bed everyday not working, not helping me with the bills, and he has the nerve to have a limp dick every time I want to fuck! I can go on," Lisa said chuckling. "What's up with you, though?"

Lisa used to date Danielle's older cousin Tray, and despite the seven-year age difference the two had grown close. Danielle always looked at Lisa as an older sister and went to her for guidance.

"I just found out I'm pregnant."

"Well damn girl, you were just a virgin. What the hell have you been doing since we last spoke?"

"I know. I was messing with that sexy Colombian I had told you about, but then I met this Puerto Rican dude and started going out with him and now I'm pregnant."

"Oh. Girl, you're keeping it, aren't you? What did this dude have to say?"

"You know I don't believe in abortion, so yes I'm keeping the baby, and I haven't told him yet. I'm scared."

"Scared? What the fuck you scared for? If your cousin finds out, that nigga going to be scared. Give me the boy's number. I'm going to call him right now and let him know for you."

"Don't curse him out. I don't want you to scare him off!" Danielle replied, running a hand down her face in frustration.

"You are making me hate him already D, but alright. Give me his number. We are about to do a three-way."

"973-555-5252," Danielle said, as Lisa dialed the number.

After three rings, Vargas picked up.

"Hello,"

"Is this Vargas?"

"Yeah, who dis?"

"This is Lisa, Danielle's older cousin. She was just at the doctor and was told she is pregnant! Y'all need to talk about this baby situation pronto."

"Wait, did you say pregnant? What the fuck?"

"Like I just said, y'all need to talk about the baby situation. Matter of fact, where are you going to be tonight? I will bring her over."

"Oh man, this is a lot but yeah. I'll be on Montgomery Street at the carwash tonight. You can bring her by."

"I'll bring her after five," Lisa said. She hung up on Vargas as he continued to talk.

"That nigga sounds like he is slow. What the fuck were you thinking D?"

"I don't know. I thought he was cute and the sex is good."

"You sure know how to pick them. And he going to be your baby daddy? Girl, you're going to have a long road ahead if he is as dumb as he sounds."

After work, Lisa was outside in her blue Lincoln Navigator waiting for Danielle so they could head to Paterson.

"Hey girl, you ready?"

"I'm just nervous. I never expected to be pregnant. You know I always wanted to be married first before I started having kids."

"Well, you should've kept those legs closed," Lisa said with a laugh. "I'm sorry. I couldn't help myself with that comment."

Pulling up to the carwash on the corner of Montgomery Street and Lafayette, the girls saw Vargas outside with his brother Flex and one other guy.

Lisa parked her car and honked her horn signaling Vargas to come over.

As Vargas came closer to the truck, Danielle got out.

"Yo, you had your cousin call me to tell me that you're pregnant?"

"Yeah, I did." Danielle started crying.

"I know you're scared, but I'm here. We are going to get through this and I'm going to hold you and the baby down. We are going to be alright," Vargas said, making Danielle feel a little more at ease. He gave her a hug and a kiss on the cheek.

Danielle hopped back into the truck with Lisa with tears rolling down her face.

"So, what happened?" Lisa asked, as she pulled away from the curb.

Sniffling she replied, "He said everything was going to be okay, so I'm going to trust him."

They arrived outside of Danielle's place.

"Thank you, Lisa," Danielle said, as she exited the truck.

"No problem, baby. Call me if you need me."

Danielle entered her room and fell on her knees crying until she couldn't cry anymore.

During her first trimester, Danielle moved in with Vargas who was staying at his godmother's house on North Fourth Street near Haledon Avenue. At first, Danielle was happy being with him, but as time went on, he hung out more and more with his boys, spending less and less time with her. When she had her prenatal appointments he never wanted to get up and go with her. Danielle started to feel alone. She realized she really didn't know Vargas. Yes they had great sex, but after the sex was done, they had nothing in common and she wasn't happy.

She was ready to leave. The apartment had roaches and was overcrowded since his godmother Maggie had three kids. It also bothered her that Vargas showed Maggie, who he met after Danielle, more attention than he did her. Danielle's family in North Carolina told her to move closer to them, and she was now willing to take them up on their offer. She wasn't about to have a baby living in any type of poor conditions.

She informed Vargas, who seemed very nonchalant about her moving—which bothered her— but she figured they needed a break from each other for a while and maybe it would improve their relationship.

After a few months living with her grandmother, Grandma Lilly, and her Great Grandmother Essie in North Carolina, Danielle was ready to go back to New Jersey. Danielle was raised in the same house as her grandma and great grandma for most of her life, but her grandma could be very hard to deal with and Danielle was ready to leave. She was now six months pregnant. When she spoke to Vargas he sounded as if he missed her.

"I miss you, baby."

"I miss you too, but if you want to go date other people, I will be ok with that," Danielle said on the other end of the phone.

"Nah babe, I don't want anyone else. Just try to come back soon. I got to go, but I love you."

"I love you too," Danielle said before hanging up.

Two weeks prior she found out she was having a girl. She was starting to get more excited about becoming a mother. She had come up with a plan to surprise Vargas and move back to New Jersey the following week.

It was the second weekend in May. Danielle hopped on a Greyhound from Charlotte, North Carolina to Newark, New Jersey. Michelle picked her up from Newark's Penn Station and took her to Maggie's house. When they pulled up to the house, the door was open because the kids were outside playing in the street. Danielle walked right in excited to see Vargas, especially since she was surprising him. As she walked toward the kitchen, she heard noises coming from his room. *What the hell is that?* she wondered. She slowly and quietly opened the door. To her surprise she saw Vargas on top of a short, pretty Puerto Rican, grinding the shit out of her. Danielle screamed. Vargas turned and saw Danielle and pulled his dick out of the girl. Danielle ran outside on the front porch and started crying.

Vargas got off Tisha, who was his new girlfriend, and threw on some sweatpants and went after Danielle.

"What the fuck are you doing here?" Vargas questioned Danielle when he saw her crying on the porch.

"Are you serious? I came to see my man, only to find you're fucking another bitch and you're asking me what I am doing here? I'm six months pregnant with your baby and this is what you do to me?"

"You weren't here so I moved on. You expected me to wait for you?"

Danielle couldn't believe what had just come out of Vargas's mouth. With a disgusted look she said, "I just spoke to you last week, and I told you that you could see other people. You told me you didn't want anyone else and that you loved me. You are such a fucking liar. All you had to do is be honest and I wouldn't have wasted my time coming up here trying to surprise you. You are a piece of shit."

"Whatever yo, that's my new girlfriend and I have been seeing her for a month anyway."

Danielle was extremely hurt. She wanted to fuck Vargas's life over so he could feel her pain.

"And where the hell is all my shit?" she asked.

"It's inside in the hallway closet."

Danielle came up with an idea.

25

"Let me go get some of my things and call Michelle to pick me up."

"Sure, whatever. The phone is on the kitchen table," Vargas replied.

First, Danielle called Michelle and told her to come back and pick her up. After she hung up with Michelle, Danielle called the Paterson Police Department and pressed three for the warrant squad. She knew Vargas had a warrant for non-payment of child support for his other two kids.

"Hello, Sgt. Warren. Warrant squad, how can I help you?"

"Hello, I'm calling because you have a warrant out on Jose Vargas, DOB 02/16/1981. Well, he is here at 72 North Fourth Street, first floor."

"Hold on ma'am, let me just verify if he has an active warrant."

Danielle was put on hold for a half a minute.

"Yes, ma'am we have him here in our system. We will be arriving at the residence shortly."

Danielle hung up. She walked back to the front room by the front door. "Michelle, will be here shortly to pick me up," Danielle told him. Vargas went back into the room with Tisha as Danielle waited on the sofa in the living room for ten minutes.

BOOM BOOM BOOM at the front door.

"Police, open up!" A man shouted through the door.

Danielle opened the door. "He is in his room officer," Danielle said, as she walked toward Vargas's room.

Danielle opened the door to see Vargas and Tisha fucking again.

"What the fuck?" Vargas shouted.

"Mr. Vargas, we are gonna need you to put on some clothes

and come with us," said the tall, slim, brown and gray-haired Caucasian officer.

Danielle closed the door so Vargas and Tisha could get dressed. When Vargas stepped out of the room, the officers arrested him, and took him away in an unmarked car.

Tisha was surprised. She couldn't believe all that was going on.

Maggie walked up to Danielle. "I know that was you that called the police! I can't believe you had the police come and arrest him because he didn't want to be with you!" she yelled in her squeaky voice.

"I didn't care if he wanted to be with me or not, it was him lying. I wasted money I could have used for my baby. I moved back up here because he said he loved me and wanted to be with me."

"Well, you didn't have to put him in jail! So I need you to go outside and wait for Michelle to pick you up."

"Ok whatever," Danielle said, as she sucked her teeth and rolled her eyes.

Tisha came outside and sat next to Danielle on the steps.

"Hey, I'm so sorry. I didn't know what was going on. He told me he had a baby on the way, but that you two had broken up."

"He lied. We never broke up, I just moved to North Carolina. We still talked on the phone, he still said he loved me and wanted to be together."

"I didn't know," Tisha said, as she stood up and walked down the steps to head home. "I'm so sorry."

Michelle pulled up in her white, 2000 two-door Honda Accord a few moments later and Danielle hopped in. As they drove off, Danielle told Michelle all that had happened.

Danielle had been staying with Michelle since the incident with Vargas. Vargas's middle brother Ace, who was now dating Michelle, had bailed Vargas out after Danielle begged him to since she felt sorry for having him locked up. Vargas stayed cordial with Danielle for the sake for the baby, but he moved on with another girl named Mona soon after being released. Mona was skinny, with dark brown skin and a moon pie face. She was two years younger than Danielle and had a three-year-old daughter. Mona was a stripper, and everyone knew her because she would trick for money if she needed to in order to make ends meet.

One hot summer night in July, Danielle, who was already a week past her due date, was playing UNO with Michelle and a few of Michelle's friends, when suddenly her water broke. Michelle rushed Danielle to Holy Name Hospital in Teaneck. After Danielle was settled in her room, Michelle left to go pick up Vargas so he could be there for the birth of his daughter. Vargas spent the night with Danielle in the hospital and stayed until she gave birth to their daughter, Naja Vargas. Naja was 8 pounds, 6 ounces. Vargas was excited and after the birth he went home to celebrate with his boys. Danielle thought since Naja was the only child of his he'd actually seen come into the world, he would love her the most and would finally want to become a family. However, that dream was never to become a reality.

Shortly after Naja was born, things started to crumble. Danielle moved back to Teaneck with her Aunt Lorraine, but still had some unresolved issues in Paterson she wanted to handle. While Danielle was pregnant with Naja, Vargas's girlfriend

Mona had threatened her. *Bitch, I will kick that baby out of your stomach.* Now that Naja was out of her stomach, Danielle was ready to confront her.

It was now November 2002. Vargas wanted Danielle to drop off Naja, now four months old, so he could spend time with her. Vargas and Mona were staying at their friend's house at the Tower's, a well-known apartment complex in Paterson. Danielle dropped Naja off for only a few hours. Mona wasn't there and that's who Danielle really wanted to see.

The next day, Danielle thought of how she was going to get to Mona.

"Hey, what's up Shante?" Danielle said, after Shante picked up the phone.

"Nothing much, just bored. What's up?"

"I need a ride over to Paterson. I need to go to the Tower's. I left Naja's bottle over at her dad's place."

Danielle had plenty of bottles but needed an excuse to go by Vargas's so she could run into Mona.

When Danielle and Shante arrived at the apartment, Danielle told Shante to stay in the car with the baby and she would be right back. Danielle entered the last building that was on the corner of West Broadway. She walked up the four steps that led up to apartment 1-D.

Danielle rang the bell. Vargas answered.

"What's up Danielle. What do you want?"

"I left one of Naja's bottles here last night. I came to get it."

"Danielle, I didn't see no bottle, but let me go get Mona because she wants to see you anyway."

Danielle stood in the hallway waiting for Mona to come out. When Mona appeared at the door, she had a bag in her hand.

29

Danielle didn't think much of it.

"I'm here, bitch. Kick my stomach now," Danielle said to Mona.

Mona swung the bag in her hand and hit Danielle in the head, but Danielle's adrenaline was so high, she never felt it.

After Mona swung the bag, Danielle punched her in the face causing her to trip and fall in the middle of the hallway. Danielle ran over to her and started kicking her.

"Who is kicking who now, bitch?" Danielle yelled, while she continued to kick and stomp her.

"Vargas, get her off me!" Mona shouted.

A crowd had started to form. Vargas was taking this all in. He had two girls fighting over him, but Danielle was really fighting because Mona disrespected her and her baby.

Vargas ran over, grabbed Danielle and started to push her out the building. Danielle was still yelling shit to Mona on the way out. Then Danielle saw blood all over Vargas's shirt.

"Vargas, what the fuck? You're bleeding. Did that bitch cut you?"

"No, motherfucker, that's you. You're bleeding!"

Danielle touched her head and blood was all over her hand.

Mona had a steel pipe in the bag that she had swung at Danielle. It opened a deep gash on the right side of Danielle's forehead.

Danielle was even more furious. Once Vargas got her out the building, she got back in Shante's car.

"OMG, Danielle, you have a hole in your head. What happened to you?" Shante asked, as she hurried to pull out of the parking lot.

"I really came over here to fuck Mona up. That bitch hit me

with a steel pipe. Take me to St. Joe's. I got to go get stitches."

Shante was in disbelief, but she knew Danielle was a firecracker.

"How was Naja?"

"She slept the whole time," Shante answered.

Danielle looked back at Naja, who was sound asleep.

Danielle then thought about what just happened,

How the hell do you hit me with a pipe and still get your ass whooped? Danielle said to herself laughing, as Shante pulled up to the emergency room.

Chapter 3

A year and half passed and Danielle was back in Charlotte, North Carolina, but this time she went to go live with her other aunt, Tina. Tina was the second oldest after her mom. She was cool but could change up on you at the drop of a dime. Tina had one son, Jerry. Soon as he graduated high school, he joined the Air Force and barely stayed in contact with the family. Tina had a two-bedroom apartment. Grandma Lily and her Great Grandma Essie had sold their five-bedroom home and moved in with Tina, so when Danielle moved in, she slept in the living room on a futon. Danielle had sent Naja, who was now almost two, to go live with her mom in Raleigh so she could save money. Danielle got a job at WEST, which was a third-party vendor to businesses like Cingular, Walgreens and other companies, and they handled the customer service calls. While in North Carolina, Michelle contacted Danielle and told her Vargas had gotten locked up and was going to go away for a while due to drug charges, and he wanted Danielle to write him.

Danielle had no intention of getting back with Vargas, but for the sake of her daughter she would write him a letter so they could have peace with one another. She wrote Vargas a short letter, giving him her address and told him she was letting their daughter stay with her mom until she saved enough money to head back to New Jersey.

Vargas wrote her back and told her he and Mona had broken up, that he missed her and she was his real ride or die. Six months into his two-year sentence, the two had gotten back together. Danielle was writing him two to three letters a day. In his letters he was writing everything Danielle wanted to hear—even that he wanted to marry her. He even tattooed her name on his arm while in jail to prove to her he was serious.

Vargas had another year and a half to do. In that time Danielle left North Carolina and moved back to Paterson with a white girl named Samantha, who had grown up with Vargas and he called his cousin. Danielle was now in the middle of the hood on Twelfth and East Twenty-Second. Danielle was now closer to Vargas and would take a bus on the weekends from Newark to go see him in Allendale.

Danielle was living in a drug infested area. She had dope addicts roaming her apartment hallway all the time and Samantha was constantly letting the local drug dealers chill in the apartment. It was like a party house all the time. Danielle didn't feel comfortable in her own home most days. In the meantime, Danielle found a full-time job as a receptionist at an OB/GYN office in Englewood.

Danielle saved enough money and rented an apartment on the corner of East Twenty-Third and Eighth Avenue. She was happy she had found a place, especially since now Vargas had somewhere to go when he came home.

After Vargas was released, everything was great between the two. Danielle's mom dropped Naja off to her, however she was not pleased her daughter continued to stay in Paterson and live in poor surroundings and was even more unhappy that she was back with Vargas. However, her mother couldn't force her to see how naïve she was.

After two months, Vargas was back to his old habits and on top of that, Danielle found herself pregnant again. Vargas told her he didn't want any more kids. He was constantly cheating on her and wouldn't watch Naja when she went to work. He would say: *he wasn't a babysitter.* Danielle was stressed to the max. She was paying all the bills and walking from her apartment to East Twenty-Seventh and Fourteenth Avenue every morning to drop Naja off at the babysitter. Vargas was always out, only came home when he felt like it, and constantly ignored her phone calls.

One evening Danielle, who couldn't cook, looked up a new recipe for dinner: breaded pork chops, string beans with rice and gravy. She only had five dollars to her name and she spent our dollars getting the groceries she needed from the bodega across the street. She made Vargas a plate and sent him a text to tell him she had made him dinner and would leave it in the microwave for him when he came in that night. Danielle fed Naja and after watching some TV, they both dozed off. Danielle never got a reply from Vargas. Three days passed and he still hadn't come home. Danielle was a mess. She cried every day he didn't return home; she was tired and hurt. On the fourth day she threw the plate of food in the garbage. She spent her last few dollars to make him a home cooked meal and he returned the favor by not coming home and never calling her. When Danielle got home that evening, she called the local hospital, the police department and the Passaic County Jail. Vargas was in none of those places, so she then went through the T-Mobile phone bill that Vargas had in her name and that she was paying for. She called every number she didn't recognize to see if she could find him or have someone relay a message for him to come home. Danielle felt like a fool. She had a man who disappeared on her, a three-year-old, one on the way and one dollar in her bank account. Danielle was so stressed that she started smoking cigarettes and Black & Mild's, despite knowing it was harmful to the baby. She was hurt and didn't care. She didn't know how she was going to pay the next month's rent and was three months behind on the electric bill.

Five days had passed since Vargas had been home, and while sitting near the window crying with Naja in her arms, Danielle heard keys opening the front door. Vargas finally made his way home.

"Where the fuck have you been?" Danielle yelled, soon as she saw his face come through the door.

"Hey babe, my bad, I got locked up," Vargas said to her in a calm voice, trying to defuse the situation.

"You're a fucking liar. I called the jail and the police department!"

"Did you call Bergen County? Because that was where I was at. I was in the car with Flex and Chino and the cops pulled us over on Route Four. I had an old warrant in Elmwood Park and they took me in."

"So you got arrested, and Flex and Chino didn't call or come

35

over to let me know that so that I wouldn't go crazy and start worrying?"

"I'm sorry babe, but I'm here now."

Danielle knew he was lying because Flex would've called her or answered her phone calls.

She wanted to believe him, so she let it go.

A week passed and everything seemed to be going good between Vargas and Danielle. The arguing had stopped. Vargas started to watch Naja, which helped Danielle get to work on time and to save more money.

"Bae, Diablo and I are going to the city to get some product to move. Do you have four hundred dollars? I'm going to flip it and give you back double."

"The only four hundred dollars I have is for the rent, which is due in a few days."

"I promise, I got you. I'm going to make it better for us."

Danielle gave Vargas the four hundred dollars she had saved up for half the rent.

The next day after Danielle got out of work, she called Vargas to check and see how the transaction went with him and Diablo.

"Hey babe, did you guys get back?"

"I was just about to call you. You're not going to believe what happened," Vargas said on the other end of the phone.

"We went to go meet these guys after we paid them and got the product. We realized they gave us crushed white chocolate, and when we told them and asked for our money back, they pulled a gun on us. We ran to the car and they chased us until we lost them," Vargas said.

"What? I gave you our rent money. You need to get my

money back. Have Diablo give you back what you lost."

"I'll talk to Diablo."

"Talk? You need to man up and tell him to give you the fucking money back!" Danielle screamed as she hung up the phone.

Danielle couldn't wrap her head around Vargas's story. It didn't make sense. Why would Vargas take their rent money, risking his own child to be cast out in the street. Danielle was beyond pissed, but what could she do? She took the story for what it was, but now she had to find four hundred dollars in three days to make up for the missing rent money.

Later that night Vargas came home and told her Diablo wouldn't give him the money because he had lost his money too. That only angered Danielle more. She had to think of something and fast.

At the office where Danielle worked, they did abortions. The next day a woman happened to come in for an abortion and paid four hundred and fifty dollars in cash. Danielle took this as her chance to take the money. She filed the patient's chart back so that accounting wouldn't notice the missing money. When the patient returned for her follow-up visit the following week, Danielle would get the file for the doctor and file it back so nobody would realize the money was missing.

Danielle had marked the patient's follow-up appointment down so nobody would find out what she did. The appointment was for Monday, December 6, 2003.

Danielle was now twelve weeks pregnant and still trying to wrap her head around all the drama she was going through with Vargas. They already had Naja and she was barely keeping her head above water. She was doing things out of character such as stealing so her family could survive.

Danielle dreamed of being married, living in a house with a white fence and having kids in that order—but that wasn't her reality. She would never achieve her dreams with someone like Vargas who only cared about himself.

A week passed, and it was now Sunday, December 5th. Danielle knew the next day she had to put her plan into action so her job wouldn't find out about the stolen money.

Meanwhile, Vargas had been cheating and started to feel guilty, especially since he lost the rent money and Danielle was pregnant with their second baby. When he came in that night after being on the block all day, he took Naja, who was lying next to Danielle, and placed her in her crib. He laid down next to Danielle and started kissing on her neck. Danielle woke up and told him she had work in the morning and needed to get some sleep. However, Vargas kept on kissing on her neck, then her shoulder and kept going down until he got to her pussy. He knew once he worked his tongue on her clit, her complaining would turn into moaning. Vargas knew her well because soon after she was moaning, and after eating her out, he stuck his dick in her, fucking her missionary and doggy style. Danielle then rode his dick until she came. They rested for an hour and started fucking again before they both fell asleep. Danielle was tired but had to get up for work. However when she got out of the shower, Vargas came in the bathroom, bent her over and started fucking her again while she held on to the sink. After he finished nutting on her back, Danielle was forty-five minutes behind schedule. Danielle decided to stay home with him. She somehow convinced herself she wouldn't get caught and called out of work and they ended up fucking all day.

The next day Danielle returned to work. After sitting at her desk for five minutes, the office manager Rachael came in and asked Danielle to come with her to the back office.

"Danielle, there have been complaints that you have been rude on the phone, late for work on numerous occasions and a patient came in yesterday and said when she came in for her initial appointment, she paid you four hundred and fifty dollars in cash. However, there is no record of it and her chart was filed back."

"I have never been rude, and I was only late once. And as far as the patient and the money, I don't know what you're talking about," Danielle lied.

"Well, Dr. Lee told me that I have to let you go. I'm sorry," Rachael said.

Danielle had only been late once and was never rude to anyone on the phone. She knew it had to do with the missing money, but since they had no real proof she stole it, they had to fire her for other reasons.

Danielle was pissed off at herself. If she had just went to work the previous day she would still have her job. But no, she wanted to stay home and fuck the same person who put her in this predicament in the first place.

Danielle cried the whole way home. She texted Vargas that she got fired because she had to steal money to replace the money he lost. He never answered.

Vargas never came home that night and all her texts and calls went unanswered.

The next day she filed for unemployment. In the meantime, she tried her best to put a smile on for her baby girl.

Vargas lost her money and caused her to get fired. She

believed all of his lies and he couldn't be bothered to even call or text her back, check on the baby or on her, and she had no more money.

This couldn't be her life. She hated it. She packed Naja an overnight bag, put her jacket on and strapped her in the stroller. Danielle walked Naja to Park Avenue and East Nineteenth where she saw Vargas laughing it up with some of his boys.

"Oh, you want to hang out with these motherfuckers, while I'm at home waiting for you. You couldn't even call to check in on me and Naja."

"What do you mean? I'm out here grinding."

"Well grind out here with your daughter. You can take her for a little while and you can bring her back when you decide to come home. Her diapers, cup and an extra pair of clothes are in her bag."

"What the fuck?"

Danielle walked off leaving Naja in the stroller next to Vargas.

Vargas screamed her name over and over until she couldn't hear him anymore.

Danielle returned home and felt like she just wanted to end her life. All she wanted was for Vargas to love and respect her. She thought when she had Naja it would make Vargas love her more and make him want to do his best to provide for his family. But that wasn't happening. She was broke and had an even more broke baby daddy who sold drugs but never had any real money to show for it.

Danielle went into the kitchen and got a knife. She started to cut down her wrist next to the green vein. She knew if she cut the vein, she would die a long, messy, uncomfortable death. Her blood was leaking off her wrist dripping onto the floor. Danielle decided to call Michelle. Danielle knew if she committed suicide, nobody would find her right away. Her body would be rotting in the apartment until someone smelled the stench of a decaying body and she didn't want that.

"Hey, Danielle," Michelle answered.

With tears running down her face, Danielle said, "Michelle, I want to die. I hate my life."

"What? What happened?"

Danielle explained all that had happened.

"Where is Naja?"

"I took her to the block and left her with Vargas."

"Danielle, stop it! You're pregnant, you have Naja, you have a lot to live for. I will call 911 for an ambulance to come take you to the hospital if you're having suicidal thoughts."

"No, don't call them. I just need to feel wanted."

"Danielle, you have me and Shante. We are your friends. We love you. Call Vargas and get your baby back and get yourself together. Everything will work out. If you're still feeling down, I'll come over later once I'm finished at work."

Once Michelle hung up, Danielle dried her eyes and called Vargas.

"What do you want, you crazy ass bitch?" Vargas said, when he finally answered the phone.

"I need you to bring Naja back home."

"You are fucking unstable. I'm not bringing her back."

"That's my baby. You don't do shit for her. Bring my baby back, you piece of shit."

"Suck my dick!" Vargas said, as he hung up in her ear.

Danielle called Michelle back to tell her Vargas didn't want to bring Naja back.

Michelle had her own issues going on. She had just given birth to her son, who she had with Ace, and unbeknownst to Danielle, he was cheating and beating on Michelle.

Michelle convinced Ace to contact Vargas and have him take Naja back to Danielle.

Vargas wasn't willing to see Danielle, so he had Michelle pick up Naja to take her home.

Danielle felt as if she was starting to lose herself. She came from a decent family and grew up in a nice house, in a nice town. How did she ever stoop so low to be with someone who had nothing, and pretty much came from nothing? How could she allow such a person to cause her to lose herself mentally and emotionally?

Two months passed since Danielle and Vargas broke up and they had no contact with each other. She was evicted from her apartment and moved back to Teaneck with her Aunt Lorraine, her husband Terry and their one-year-old son Junior. Danielle had her mother take Naja again for a little while since the doctors informed her that she couldn't lift anything if she wanted to continue to have a healthy pregnancy—despite the fact she was still smoking.

One morning Danielle was in bed and felt cramping in her lower abdomen. She decided to get up and take a hot shower. While in the shower, the cramps intensified. When she stepped out of the shower, she felt a gushing of water pour down her leg. She frantically called her aunt.

"JP Morgan, how can I direct your call?"

"Auntie, it's me, Danielle. I think my water broke but I'm only sixteen weeks. What do you think I should do? Call my doctor or the ambulance?"

"Oh, my goodness. I think you should call your doctor immediately, then call me back and tell me what he said."

Danielle dialed her doctor who was in Paterson.

"Dr. Nunez's office, how can I help you?"

"Hello, I am a patient there and I am four months pregnant, and I think my water just broke."

"Hold on, let me go talk to the doctor. What is your name and date of birth?"

"Danielle Lee, 9/15/1981."

Danielle waited for a few seconds for the nurse to come back on the line.

"Ms. Lee, Dr. Nunez said to come in right away."

"I'm in Teaneck and I have no car, so I'll be there as fast as I can."

"Okay Ms. Lee, we will see you when you get here."

Danielle had to take two buses to Paterson. She waited for the first bus. It seemed like forever, but the New Jersey Transit 756 bus finally came. Twenty-five minutes later it arrived at the Garden State Plaza Mall. Then she waited for the second bus that would drop her off right in front of the doctor's office. Meanwhile, her contractions were coming back-to-back and her pants were soaking wet. She waited for another twenty minutes until the 770 finally came. Danielle had nobody to call to help her, so she had to accomplish this mission by herself.

When Danielle finally arrived at the doctor's office, they made her sit for thirty minutes before the doctor saw her. Her water continued breaking, and not only were her pants soaked, but so was the chair she was sitting in.

When the doctor finally examined her, he told her it didn't look good.

"Ms. Lee, it seems like your body aborted the baby, and even if I could keep the baby alive and you carry to full-term, the baby would be brain dead. I need you to go across the street to St. Barnet's hospital so you can be admitted for delivery. I'm so sorry for your loss."

Danielle felt as if God just wanted to continue punishing her. If it wasn't one thing, it was another.

The hospital was expecting her and took her to her room immediately.

She undressed and they started her on Pitocin to help open the cervix.

Two hours later she pushed out a dead fetus. The nurse asked if she wanted to hold the baby and she did. The baby was so small and looked almost transparent. Danielle could see all the veins and the heart through the skin. The baby was the size of her palm. The vagina lips were evident, letting her know it was a girl since she hadn't found out yet. The nurse placed a hat on the baby's head, took pictures of the baby and gave them to Danielle. Then she put the baby's feet in black ink and stamped them on a certificate stating her time of birth and time of death, along with a sympathy poem.

Danielle cried until her release the next evening. Danielle realized she should have never held the baby and the fact that she had nobody to console her only made her cry more. This was a time she really needed someone to be there for her and she had nobody.

Danielle returned to her aunt's house. Her uncle Terry asked her where she was.

"Where the hell were you yesterday?"

"I didn't feel good, so I went to the hospital."

"Well, you aren't that sick if you're up watching TV. I need you to go to take those bags of garbage out."

"I just told you I didn't feel well, so I'm not taking the garbage out."

"Excuse me, this is my house and I'm allowing you to stay here, so you need to get your ass up and take that garbage out."

Danielle was getting pissed off. She couldn't tell him the truth because she knew he would kick her out if he found out that she had gotten pregnant again. Terry was mean but he knew Danielle could be much smarter with her decisions if she just used her God-given senses. She had a baby with a piece of shit which was highly disappointing, and if she made that mistake again living in his house, she had to go. *You can be stupid once, but if you keep being stupid you deserve what you get served,* he always said.

"Well, to tell you the truth, I was pregnant and had a miscarriage. I had to give birth yesterday and I'm still bleeding heavy. That's why I cannot take your garbage out right now."

"You what? Does your aunt know about this? Oh hell no, you gotta go. I told your ass not to get pregnant again. You don't fucking listen."

Terry stormed into the kitchen to call Lorraine. Danielle went to go eavesdrop on his conversation.

"You had Danielle in my house pregnant and didn't tell me? I don't give a fuck, L. She has to go, and she has to go today."

Danielle went back into the living room before Terry caught her listening and started crying. After he hung up, he walked past her.

"You better find somewhere to go because you aren't staying

45

here." He then walked upstairs to his bedroom and slammed the door.

Danielle's phone rang. She answered.

"Danielle, I told you to stay in your room and relax. Why would you go in the living room? I told you not to tell him about the baby. I had it all worked out, but you messed everything up now."

"I know. I wanted to watch TV and he told me to take those heavy bags out to the garbage and I wasn't going to do it."

"Well, now you have to leave. He isn't trying to hear anything else. I did my best to help you, but your mouth got you in trouble, and now he is mad at me. I'll talk to you later. I got to get back to work."

Danielle looked through her contacts in her phone. She couldn't call Michelle because she was staying on someone's couch with her son because she had lost her apartment as well. Shante was still living at home with her grandparents. There was only one person that could possibly help her, a childhood friend from church that she stayed in touch with named Tierra.

The phone rang and there was no answer. Danielle left a message hoping Tierra would call her back very soon.

Two hours passed before Tierra called back.

"Hey Danielle, I got your message. What's up?" Tierra said on the other end of the phone.

"Hey, I need a favor if you can help. I had a miscarriage and got home from the hospital today. My uncle found out I was pregnant again and he kicked me out. I was wondering if I could stay with you for a few weeks until I find somewhere else to go."

"Damn girl, that's messed up. If you don't mind sleeping on the floor in my daughter's room, you're more than welcome to stay at my house."

"That's fine. Thanks Tierra, I appreciate it."

"Do you have a car or need me to pick you up?"

"I need you to pick me up, if you don't mind."

"Ok, I get out of work at six. I have to run home really quick and should get to Teaneck by 6:30 PM. I live in Bergenfield, so I'm less than ten minutes away."

"Thank you so much. I'll see you later."

Danielle was relieved she had somewhere to go.

****

After dropping the twins off at their private school, Danielle broke down and cried. She was reminiscing about when she lost her baby, how she had nobody and how she remained so stupid for so long when it came to Vargas. Then she laughed thinking she would've kicked herself out of the house too, knowing what she knew now.

Danielle was now a beautiful, smart entrepreneur who started her own business when she lived in a cramped, two-bedroom apartment after she had the twins. After her and Stefan got serious, he invested in her business and they were now the President and CEO of PLUSH & LUSH SKIN and HAIR PRODUCTS. They had a little over ten employees. Danielle had a personal assistant named Tanisha who had become like a sister. PLUSH & LUSH had been featured in popular magazines. They had been guests on *Good Morning America* and *The View,* and had their line of products in brick and mortar stores such as Wal-Mart and Target. Danielle had come a long way from that lost young girl she once was.

Danielle continued to reminisce as she headed to her office.

****

2005

One year had passed since Danielle lost her baby. She had been reunited with Naja and hadn't heard from Vargas during that year. One day out of the blue, Vargas called her to check on Naja and asked her what happened to their baby. After telling him about the miscarriage he instantly blamed her for losing their baby.

"If you weren't stressing about me, you wouldn't have lost the baby," he said.

"No, if you weren't stressing me out, that wouldn't have never happened. But that's neither here nor there. I'm still trying to recover and talking about it won't make my baby come back."

Vargas had gotten back with Mona, but he and Danielle started fucking again shortly after he called her. Sex was the only thing they did together that flowed well. Vargas ended up dumping Mona, and he and Danielle got back together. Soon after, Danielle and Naja moved in with him in a room he was renting from a woman named Lisa. Lisa had a four-bedroom apartment on North Fourth Street in Paterson. At first, all was well with Danielle and Vargas. Lisa's younger daughter Tay would watch Naja and cared for her like a baby sister. Before long, things between Vargas and Danielle started to go downhill. Vargas started hanging out late and not spending time with her and Naja. Since Danielle still wasn't working, he would

48

give her a fifty dollar a week allowance so she could get things for Naja. In June, the Annual Puerto Rican Parade was happening in New York City. Danielle figured since she and Vargas lived together, he would go with her and Naja as a family. That wasn't the case. He gave Danielle an extra fifty dollars and told her to go have fun, and he was going with his brother and a few of his boys. Danielle was crushed. *How can he just diss us and leave me to go to a parade by myself with a four-year-old?* she thought. She was really starting to get tired of his bullshit. Soon after, things took a turn for the worse. One night, Danielle was in the house drinking with Lisa's oldest daughter Zee. Danielle wasn't much of a drinker, but Zee told her to try the bottle of Mad Dog 20/20 she had brought.

"Vargas is so fucked up. You are always in the house with the baby and he just leaves y'all to go out. He never takes you out or does anything with y'all," Zee said hotly, as she poured a drink from the bottle.

"I know. I don't know what his problem is," Danielle sighed.

"You wait up for him every night. Girl, you better than me. I would've left him by now," Zee chuckled.

Danielle started to feel stupid. She had been through so much with him and he never showed her that he appreciated her. She would leave and then come right back to him. Vargas knew that all he had to do was eat her out, give her some good dick, and he would have her wrapped around his finger. He knew he didn't have to go out of his way for her or even show her that he loved her because she would always come back to him, which made it so easy for him have his cake and eat it too.

That night Vargas got home around 1:30 AM. Danielle was still up waiting for him on the living room couch as usual, however this time she was drunk from drinking the whole bottle of Mad Dog.

"You still up, D?" Vargas said, as he walked through the living room toward Lisa's son Michael's room. When Vargas was out with other females and didn't want to be bothered with Danielle, he would sleep in the room with Michael, who was also one of his good friends.

"I was waiting for you. Why are you walking to Michael's room? I'm horny and I want to fuck!" Danielle answered, slightly slurring her words.

"Yo, I'm tired. I'm going to bed. Go upstairs, you're drunk as hell."

She got up in his face. "What the fuck you mean, you tired? Bring your ass upstairs and go to bed with me."

"Yo, chill the fuck out. I'm not in the mood to fuck."

Danielle was already upset; she wanted his time and he never gave it to her, and now she wanted to fuck and have him kiss and hold her. Danielle just felt so much rage that she bawled her hand up in a fist and started punching him. She wasn't paying attention as she was throwing punches. One of the punches landed in his face. After she realized what she did, she backed up and he turned around and pushed her so hard she fell back onto Lisa's glass coffee table and shattered it.

Everyone in the house woke up.

"What the fuck is going on?" Lisa shouted, as she came downstairs and saw Danielle laying on top of a pile of broken glass that was once her coffee table.

"This bitch is crazy," Vargas said. "She punched me in my face because I didn't want to fuck her. I'm calling Ace and I'm going to let him handle it."

50

Danielle was still in shock as to what just happened. She got up off the floor careful not to cut herself with any of the glass that surrounded her. Naja was woken out of her sleep and everyone was up shaking their head as her and Vargas argued. Ten minutes later, Ace was at the door. He walked in the living room.

"What the fuck happened? It's two in the morning and you called me over here."

"This crazy ass bitch punched me in my face because I didn't want to fuck."

"Why the fuck you punch my brother? I am not him. I will fuck you up!" Ace yelled at Danielle.

"Yo, shut the fuck up. This has nothing to do with you. You need to go back home and mind your own damn business!" Danielle shouted in response.

"This is my brother. He called me, and this is my business. I will knock you the fuck out."

Danielle was getting pissed off. She went to go punch Ace in the face, but he came around and hooked her from the other side, busting her lip.

Michael grabbed him just in case he tried to hit Danielle again.

"I'm going to need you to get the fuck out of my house," Lisa told Ace.

Ace left and the commotion settled. Danielle went upstairs to go to sleep, while Vargas went to Michael's room and slept.

When Vargas woke up the next morning his right eye was black. He went upstairs to wake up Danielle.

"Yo, wake up! You see what the fuck you did to me? I got a fucking black eye. I got to walk around and tell people my girl

51

did it. You are a fucking nutcase."

"You're a piece of shit. Who the fuck has their brother confront their girl and have him bust her lip?" Danielle said, as she shook her head. "But what I did was wrong so I will apologize. But you're paying for Lisa's table."

Five months passed. Danielle and Vargas broke up again. Vargas had been the perfect boyfriend for about two weeks after the fight, but then went right back to staying out late and most likely cheating. Danielle couldn't prove it, but it was her gut instinct.

Danielle really had nowhere to go. She ended up going into a shelter on Circle Avenue in Paterson. Vargas still stayed in contact with her because of Naja. He would tell Danielle that he wanted to be with her, but that he had met someone else. Vargas started dating a Rosa Parks High School senior named Glory. Glory was about five-six, 130 pounds, light skinned and Puerto Rican with long black hair and big, bug eyes. Danielle wasn't jealous because she knew Vargas would come back to her.

Vargas was living with his godmother Maggie once again, who now lived on Bridge Street.

"Vargas, Naja wants to come visit you for the weekend."

"I won't be home until late, but you can drop her off. Maggie will be home."

Danielle dropped Naja off for the weekend and also wanted Naja to bring back information.

That Sunday, Danielle went to go pick up Naja.

"I'm downstairs. You can bring her down," Danielle said to Vargas, who was on the other end of the phone.

It had been a while since Danielle had seen him. She was tired of all the bullshit, but she wanted her family back and

Glory was in the way.

To Danielle's surprise, Glory brought Naja downstairs. Not Vargas.

"Hey, she ate and her stuff is in the bag," Glory said, when she got to the bottom of the stairs. Naja gave her mom a hug and waved bye to Glory. As Glory walked back up the stairs, she started laughing.

Danielle was annoyed. *Why the fuck was that bitch bringing my daughter downstairs, and what the fuck was she laughing for?* Danielle wondered.

Later that night, Danielle left Naja with one of the girls at the shelter while she went out with another girl named Angela from the shelter. She and Angela went to go chill and drink at Roberto Clememte Park on Market Street. After getting drunk, Danielle called Vargas.

"What are you doing?" she asked when he answered.

"I'm here with my girl."

Danielle didn't want to hear that. "Why the fuck did you have her bring my daughter downstairs? I don't know her like that for her to be around my daughter!"

"That's my girl and she will be around her," Vargas said.

In the background Glory shouted, "What the fuck you mean, bitch? You wasn't popping no shit when you met me. You was all up in my face being nice and trying to be my friend."

"Bitch? Who the fuck are you calling a bitch?" Danielle replied.

Danielle and Glory were going back and forth arguing. "Bitch, I will come to that shelter you live at and fuck you up."

"Bring your ass. I will fucking kill you," Danielle said, before Vargas hung up on her.

The next day Danielle knew she would fight Glory. Glory was the jumping kind, so Danielle knew she had to round up a few people she knew to come to the fight. Danielle called her friend Helena, who she hung with occasionally and lived a few blocks away from the shelter. Helena then called her friend Tamika, who was down to show up as well.

The day was getting later and later. Danielle told Helena she would call her soon as she got the call Glory was on her way.

The shelter mother that night was Sarah, a chubby white woman in her mid-thirties. All the girls loved when she worked because she gave them more freedom. Sarah was dating Midnight, a dark skinned guy in his early twenties that sold drugs on the block. Danielle always thought how his nickname fit him perfectly. While Midnight and Sarah were outside smoking a cigarette and talking, a group of kids were walking in their direction. A Latina female with cornrows and an airbrushed shirt that had GLORY painted on it walked up to them and asked if Danielle was there.

"Let me go check," Sarah answered.

While Sarah was heading back in, she saw some of the girls with Glory hide behind the shelter van that was parked near the shelter entrance.

Sarah went inside and told Renee, another single mom who lived in the shelter to go upstairs and tell Danielle there were girls outside looking for her.

Renee rushed upstairs. "Danielle, there is a group of girls outside waiting for you, and Sarah said some are hiding behind the van. I guess they want to jump you when you go outside."

Danielle had never been jumped; she knew she had to make a call ASAP for some back up.

Danielle dialed a number. After the third ring, a man with a deep voice answered.

"Hakeem, is that you?" Danielle asked.

"Yo, who dis?" he asked.

"It's Danielle."

"What's up little cuz, what's going on?"

"My baby daddy's girlfriend is outside the shelter I'm at on North Third and Circle Avenue. She has a group of girls with her and they want to jump me. Can you come over and referee?"

"Say no more, I'm on my way. I'll call you when I'm outside."

Danielle hung up and could hear Glory and her friends shouting for her to come outside.

"We know you're in there, bitch! Come outside!" someone yelled.

It wasn't long before she got the call from Hakeem.

Danielle went outside and walked toward him.

"Nobody's jumping my cousin," Hakeem said to the crowd.

"By the way," he said as he looked at Glory, "who the fuck are you?"

"Can't you read?" Pointing to her shirt, "I'm Glory."

While Glory was rolling her neck and telling Hakeem to read her shirt, Danielle placed her cellphone in Hakeem's pocket. As she did, she said, "Fuck this," and balled up her fist and punched Glory in the face.

The two girls started fighting and the crowd around them got bigger as people who were hanging outside came to see what the commotion was.

Glory got on top of Danielle and was hitting Danielle's head on the cement. As Glory was smashing Danielle's head against the ground, Danielle was thinking, *I cannot let this bitch beat my ass.* When Glory was about to smash Danielle's head against the ground for the third time, Danielle bit Glory's pinky, which was next to Danielle's mouth.

That gave Danielle a few seconds to manage to shake off Glory's grip and kick her off of her. Danielle was able to get on top of Glory and started punching her in the face.

"Bitch, I told you I was going to kill you," Danielle muttered, as she started choking Glory. Danielle's grip around Glory's neck was getting tighter and tighter. Her adrenaline was pumping and she was focused on keeping her word.

"Heeeelp, I can't breathe," Glory managed to faintly scream.

When Danielle heard that, she squeezed tighter.

Helena had finally arrived with Tamika. Helena pushed through the crowd as she could hear Glory gasping and begging for help. Helena tried to pull Danielle off Glory, but Danielle was too strong. Hakeem, who had walked off to answer a phone call, saw Danielle choking Glory, who was gasping for air. He pushed Helena out the way and grabbed Danielle off Glory just as they heard the police sirens approaching.

"Get inside the shelter now! The cops are on the corner!" Hakeem yelled.

Glory's friends had to help her up and walk her into the apartment building lobby next door to the shelter until the police dispersed the crowd and left.

Once inside, Sarah saw the knot Danielle had on her head.

"Girl, put some salt and butter on a paper towel and put on that knot. It will make it go down right away. It's an old Puerto Rican remedy," Sarah said.

The next morning when Danielle woke up the knot had

vanished, and she had ten missed calls. Danielle went to go check on Naja, who spent the night in Renee's room while the whole fighting fiasco was going on.

The phone rang.

"Hello," Danielle answered.

"Girl, I heard she got a black eye and was scared to death because she thought she was going to die," Helena said on the other end of the phone.

"Oh yeah. Well, I told her I was going to kill her. My stepfather always told me to say what you mean and mean what you say," Danielle chuckled. "But let me call you back, I got to go get Naja ready so I can take her out for lunch."

"Aight girl, call me later," Helena said, as the two hung up.

Chapter 4

It was now 2006. Danielle had a two-bedroom apartment on Summer Street. Naja always slept in the bed with Danielle, so Danielle decided to rent the second bedroom out.

Danielle decided to let Ace's new girlfriend rent the room. Her name was Bianca. Ace was still living with Michelle and dating them both. They knew Ace was dating them both, but outside of not liking each other they allowed him to do what he wanted. Danielle had met Bianca a few years prior when she was cool with Michelle. Since Bianca's baby father Trevor was from the same block Vargas and Ace hustled on, Danielle thought she was cool.

Bianca was five years younger than Danielle; she was five-one, Puerto Rican, fair skinned, petite, dyed blonde hair and around 110 pounds. She was a cute girl and very stylish. Bianca had two kids with Trevor, whom her mother had custody of, and Trevor had recently been convicted of manslaughter and was given a ten-year minimum sentence.

One evening Bianca got into an argument with one of her friends named Selena. Danielle never cared for Selena but the two were cordial. Selena came to the apartment looking for Bianca, but Bianca wasn't there. Danielle wasn't answering the door because it was late and Naja was asleep. Suddenly Danielle heard a loud boom. Then she heard someone kick in the downstairs door to her apartment.

"Her room is over there. Let's grab all that bitch's shit," Selena said to another female that accompanied her.

Danielle was laying in her bed scared. She was holding Naja, who remained asleep, hoping the two girls didn't come into her room. About ten minutes passed and the girls left. Danielle waited about five minutes before she got up to look around. She took a deep breath, then opened her bedroom door with a bat that she had in her room. Danielle entered the kitchen, looked around and saw the light in Bianca's room was still on. First Danielle went to go look at the door downstairs. The door was busted open but thankfully the deadbolt wasn't on, so she was able to still close and lock the door. She then went back upstairs into Bianca's room. Selena had taken all of Bianca's sneaker boxes, ransacked her dresser drawers and took most of her clothes. Danielle was just relieved that Selena didn't come into her room.

Danielle tried contacting Bianca but her phone was off. After getting in touch with a few people, Bianca got word and finally got in contact with Danielle. Danielle told her what happened and told her she would have to leave immediately; she couldn't risk having that kind of danger around her daughter. Danielle felt bad but the safety of her and her daughter was more important.

Soon after, Danielle started working as a security guard at John F. Kennedy High School near Union Avenue in Paterson, which was on the other side of town of where she lived. Danielle was finally doing well for herself. She no longer felt the need of being distracted by a man and knew she could hold her and Naja down on her own. Danielle even started going back to school online so she could get a degree in criminal justice and become a cop, which was now one of her main goals. In April, Danielle started dating Antonio, who was her boss at her security job. Because there was a policy against employees dating each other, the two had to keep their relationship discreet. Antonio was a handsome, tan skinned Dominican that was six years her senior. The two would sneak around town to see each other because of the risk. In May of that year, both Danielle and Antonio took the test to become Paterson Police officers. She scored an eighty-nine and he scored ninety-nine; at orientation that July, they were both in the top twenty pick.

When Danielle and Antonio arrived at orientation, he was seated in the front row since he was in the top five and she sat four rows behind him. Danielle was surprised at all the white men who were there. She didn't even know that many white people lived in Paterson because in order to get hired you had to be a Paterson resident. After two hours of filling out paperwork and listening to the orientation speaker, Danielle was notified that she qualified to move on to the next step which was being interviewed and Danielle knew she would get the job since she worked with the captain of the police department at the high school. Everything was finally going well for her. Her and Antonio were happy and she was relieved that once they both got hired as police officers, they wouldn't have to hide their relationship any longer.

Danielle's twenty-fifth birthday came that August. Antonio planned a surprise dinner for her at Toy restaurant, which was located in Gansevoort Hotel in the meat packing district in New York City. After dinner, Antonio reserved a room inside the hotel. Danielle couldn't believe it; she felt as if she went from rags to riches. The two had only been dating for four months and she wasn't in love with him at all, but she loved the way he treated her, especially since no man had ever treated her that special. Once the two got to the room, Danielle saw that rose petals where on the bed surrounded by a bunch of balloons and a bottle of Dom Perignon Champagne and two champagne glasses where on the night stand next to the bed.

Danielle cried in excitement and gave Antonio a kiss.

"Esta noche se trata de ti. Hare todo el trabajo, solo necesito que te relajes," (Tonight is all about you. I will do all the work, I just need you to relax) Antonio whispered in her ear, as he picked her up and put her on the bed.

He unbuttoned her blouse as he kissed on her neck. He then lowered the straps and pulled down her bra and he started to suck on her nipples. Danielle started to moan; as she ran her hands through his hair she got wetter and hornier. He then kissed her stomach, moving down until he got to her pussy. To tease her, he kissed her thighs, getting her more excited. Then he took the tip of his tongue and licked her pussy up and down slowly, enticing her even more.

"Relax, my love. Imma take care of you," Antonio said, right before he put his whole mouth over her pussy and started sucking on her clit. He felt the rain pouring out of her and knew he could slip his dick in her gushy pussy. He made love to her body that whole night, making her orgasm multiple times before she finally dozed off.

The next day, Antonio took Danielle to Michelle's house to pick up Naja before dropping her off home. Danielle was on cloud nine until Vargas called her later that evening.

"Hello?"

"Hey D, it's Vargas, I was calling to say belated happy birthday, I also wanted to come by see Naja if that is okay?"

Danielle let out a big sigh. "Sure, you can come by tomorrow in the afternoon."

"Alright, bet."

The next day arrived and Vargas decided to arrive at 5 PM.

"Didn't I tell you to come in the afternoon?"

"Yeah, my bad, I got caught up."

"I hope you got caught up with some child support money because your definitely way behind."

"That's all you're worried about."

"I wouldn't be if you were actually a father and had a real relationship with her, but since your simple ass can't do that, I want the money," Danielle responded.

"Who the fuck you calling simple, you stupid bitch?"

"Who the fuck you calling a bitch? You're in my house, where I take care of your daughter that you don't do shit for."

"Bitch, get the fuck out of my face. I'm a three-star general in the Bloods now and I could have you killed."

Danielle smacked Vargas in the face. He in return punched her twice in her face. Danielle saw a knife by the kitchen sink, grabbed it and stabbed him in the chest area.

"You stupid piece of shit!" Danielle screamed.

Vargas was able to run outside of the apartment before

Danielle was able to swing the knife at him again.

"I'm calling the cops on you, you crazy bitch!" Vargas yelled from outside.

Danielle ran to the living room window where Vargas was shouting from the street and threw a glass vase she had next to her couch at him but missed. She then ran into the kitchen and grabbed the first thing she saw which was bleach and tried to throw that on him, but she missed again.

"Ha, you missed; my girlfriend's dad works for the sheriff's department. I'm going to get you locked up," he taunted.

Danielle picked up her cell phone and called Michelle.

Michelle picked up after the second ring.

"Michelle, I need you to come over right away because I'm about to go to jail and need someone to come get Naja."

"Danielle, what the fuck did you do?"

"I'll explain when you get here, but hurry."

"I'm on my way."

Danielle hung up with Michelle and dialed 911.

This motherfucker think he is going to lock me up? Okay sure, we both are going to be locked up, Danielle thought as the operator picked up the phone.

"911, what's your emergency?"

"My baby father punched me in the face twice and I had to stab him. He isn't hurt, but he is outside calling the police on me, so I'm calling the police on him too."

"Ma'am, I'm sending units out to your address as we speak."

Michelle and the police arrived shortly after. Danielle had to write a report, then handed Michelle her cell phone and told her not to call or answer any calls from her mom, and hopefully she would get out soon. Out of respect for Danielle's daughter, the police didn't put handcuffs on her, but escorted her to the back seat of the cop car.

When they arrived at the police station, Danielle saw some familiar faces. They escorted her to the back for booking. While sitting on the bench, she saw Glory's dad chatting with some of the officers. *Damn. Vargas wasted no time snitching on me to his girlfriend's father*, Danielle thought to herself.

They finally placed Danielle in her cell. There were two other women in the other two cells when she arrived. One female was crying hysterically and the other woman on the end was drunk; she was only in there until her drunkenness wore off. Danielle was placed in the middle of the two.

Danielle sat on a blue plastic mat and looked around. There was a metal toilet, a window that she couldn't reach or see through and of course the metal bars. At first she wanted to cry, but crying wasn't going to free her. She wanted to go to sleep but she didn't know who had been on that blue mat before her and didn't want to lay on it. Plus, she couldn't sleep with her mind racing, wondering if her daughter was okay or how and when she was going to get out of there.

The girl in the next cell was still crying. She looked about twenty-three years old. She was skinny, had a sewn-in blonde weave, and light-brown skin. Danielle tried to make conversation so she would stop crying. *Damn bitch. Shut up. No matter how much you cry you aren't getting out,* Danielle said to herself.

"Hey, how long have you been in here?"

Sniffling, the girl answered, "Since this morning. They

raided my apartment and found drugs. They brought me and my boyfriend in. He is in the men's section on the other side. My son was home, so they had to call DYFS and my apartment was Section 8 so I know I lost that." The girl started crying again as she spoke. "My bail is $75,000 and his is $150,000. I didn't know there were drugs in my apartment. Oh my God, I can't believe this is happening," she said, as the sobbing continued.

Thankfully it wasn't the weekend, so they were all going to see the judge in the morning.

After an hour, the girl finally stopped crying and dozed off. Danielle could hear her snoring through the wall. Danielle laid back against the wall and finally fell asleep sitting up.

The morning came and the officer yelled for them to get up. They brought in a small container of apple juice and a piece of dry bread. Danielle ate her bread and used the toothbrush and toothpaste they had passed out to brush her teeth.

The officer came in and had her and the young girl Danielle secretly named "Crybaby," handcuffed and shackled at the ankles so they could go see the judge. The men had met up with them when they reached the courtroom. Danielle saw Vargas and just gave him a nasty look. When Danielle entered the courtroom, she saw Glory sitting in the front row along with some of her friends. Danielle looked at her and smirked before she turned around and faced the judge. The judge read her charges, which were second and third degree assault with a deadly weapon. He then set her bail for ten thousand dollars with no ten percent. Danielle had never legally been in trouble before and had no past record, but she received a bail with no ten percent. However, when Vargas entered the courtroom, he received a five thousand dollar bail with ten percent, meaning he only needed five hundred dollars to be released. Vargas had been in jail numerous times for drugs, driving violations, child support—which he owed to her as well—and he was a known gang member, but got a slap on the wrist. Danielle was pissed.

After everyone saw the judge, they were escorted outside to a van. They had a barrier in the middle separating the men from the females. The van was pitch black. All you heard were voices, but you couldn't see anyone's face.

They arrived at the Passaic County Jail and got logged in. The men went one way, and Danielle and Crybaby went the other. They gave Danielle a green jumpsuit and some black canvas sneakers. They made her strip naked and take her fake ponytail off her head that she had gotten done for her birthday, which was three days prior. She stood butt naked with her arms out, while the female officer checked her. Then she had to squat, cough and hold open her butt cheeks. Danielle never felt so humiliated in her life. She then got dressed and they sent her and the girl to the bullpen, which was a holding cell until they were placed into population. Crybaby found her a spot on a top bunk and started crying again. There were five other females already in there. Danielle sat on a bench they had next to the bunk bed. They informed them to take a shower, but when Danielle walked over to the shower it looked old and dirty. She said to herself, *fuck that*. Outside of the cell was a payphone. Reaching through the bars, Danielle picked up the phone and dialed her cell phone to check on Naja. A woman answered.

"Mom, is that you?" Danielle asked

"Yes, it's your mother."

Danielle was surprised to hear her mom on the other end of

the phone since she gave Michelle specific instructions not to contact her mom.

Danielle's mother continued, "We will talk later about this, but Michelle called me because someone had to get Naja because she had to go to work. I'm at your Aunt Lorraine's house now. We are trying to get you out of there, but you have to give us some time."

After sitting in the bullpen for six hours and calling her Aunt Lorraine and mom multiple times, they finally were able to get the money together to get her out, by getting a lien on Lorraine's house. Right after Danielle got off the phone, an officer announced that everyone would be placed in population shortly. Danielle wanted to get the hell out of there before that happened. Twenty minutes passed and an officer came down and told Danielle she was going home. They just had to get the paperwork ready and she would be free. Another thirty minutes passed and Danielle changed back into her clothes, got all her belongings and paperwork, and stood by the gate waiting for it to open so she could be a free woman.

Danielle could care less about Vargas. He had put her through so much over the past five years. Even though she had allowed it, she made up her mind she was done with him. Danielle had to go to court shortly after and deal with the assault charges that the State of New Jersey had brought against her. Her lawyer was able to win the case and the charges were eventually dropped. She couldn't believe how her life changed so fast. Soon after, her and Antonio broke up. He told her he needed to concentrate on his upcoming career, but the truth was that he was embarrassed that the woman he was dating was arrested for fighting with her gang-banging baby daddy.

Chapter 5

Danielle left her apartment and was allowed to move back in with her Aunt Lorraine. Danielle soon found a new job at Citibank in Englewood Cliffs, New Jersey.

On her first day at Citibank, her co-workers introduced themselves to her. Most of them were Dominican and lived in Washington Heights or the Bronx. One co-worker made her smile when he introduced himself to her.

"What's up, I'm Pedro. Welcome. By the way my birthday is a few months away on December ninth. Just wanted to give you a head up just in case you want to get me something."

Danielle laughed and thought he was kind of cute.

Pedro was five-nine, 200 pounds, with medium brown skin. He had almond-shaped eyes and smelled like Versace.

At lunch that day, Danielle was sitting outside and Pedro came over to join her.

"Where are you from?" he asked.

"I'm from Teaneck. How about you?"

"I'm from High Bridge, which is in the Bronx."

"Ok, cool. How long have you been working here?"

"For about two years. It's a pretty cool and easy job. When the winter comes, we work about thirteen hours a day since that's our busy season."

Their conversation was cut short when his phone rang. Pedro looked at the name that popped on his cell phone.

"Hey, I got to go, my girl is calling. I'll see you inside."

"Talk to you later."

Damn, should've known he had a girlfriend, she thought, as she laughed to herself as she finished her lunch.

For the next month, the two would meet outside and chat at lunch. As Danielle got more comfortable around him, she asked if he would be her date for her cousin's wedding at the end of October which was in a few weeks. Pedro agreed.

One the day of the wedding, Danielle rented a car so she could pick Pedro up and drive to the wedding. Danielle went to Elsa's, a popular Dominican salon on Teaneck Road she had been going to since she was in the eighth grade, and had the owner Mary, do her hair in a Dube. She was running behind schedule. After she left the salon, she had Pedro meet her on the Jersey side of the George Washington Bridge and she took him back to her aunt's house so she could finish getting dressed.

Once she had finished putting on her makeup, she combed her hair down, put on her black tube dress she brought from Express and walked out to the living room to get ready to leave. Pedro looked shocked.

"Damn, you look good," he said to her.

Danielle blushed as they headed out.

After her cousin's wedding ended, her family wanted to know who Pedro was and complimented them on how good they looked together. Soon after, they headed to the reception. About two hours into the reception, Pedro got a call and took it outside. Once he came back in, he told Danielle he had to leave because he had a family emergency. Danielle assumed Pedro had someone call him so he would have an excuse to leave. Danielle took him all the way back to the Bronx. Once it was time for him to exit the car, they said their goodbyes and Pedro kissed her. Danielle was caught off guard, but she kissed him back. They kissed one more time before Pedro hopped out and said he would call her. Danielle drove back to the reception in Ridgewood, New Jersey with a big smile on her face. Once the reception was over, Danielle was heading home when she got a call from Miguel. Danielle and Miguel had just recently started talking but it was nothing serious. Danielle had met Miguel a few years back when she used to hang with a girl named Inga, who she met when she would go visit Vargas at the Passaic County Jail. Inga was dating Miguel's older brother, Eddie.

Inga moved to Paterson from the Dominican Republic when she was ten. Inga and Danielle formed a close relationship after seeing each other weekly at the Passaic County Jail. The two started hanging out all the time at all of the local Dominican bars on Market Street and even dressing alike at times. Danielle caught Inga cheating on Eddie, and because at the time Danielle and Inga were renting a two-bedroom attic apartment from Eddie's family, Danielle felt Inga crossed the line and told Carlos, Eddie and Miguel's other brother. That ended the friendship between Inga and Danielle.

Miguel was five-nine, with tan skin, beautiful hazel eyes and silky black hair. Miguel had just come home from prison and saw Danielle when she walked past his cousin's barbershop when she lived on Summer Street and the two kept in touch.

"Hey Danielle, what are you doing?"

"I just left my cousin's wedding. What's up? What are you doing?"

Danielle hadn't heard from him in a couple of weeks, so she was surprised at the call.

"I'm on Market Street with my brother and my boys. Come over here if you want. We can chill."

"Yeah, I'll be over there in twenty minutes."

Danielle hopped on Route Four West and headed to Paterson.

Danielle saw Miguel and his brother Franklin standing on Market Street across from an old armory. Franklin was Danielle's age while Miguel was four years older. Miguel and Franklin looked a lot alike apart from the fact that Franklin was lighter. Danielle parked the car and walked over to Miguel. He gave her a kiss on the cheek and Franklin gave her a hug.

"You look really nice," Miguel said.

"Thank you. So, what are y'all drinking?"

"We got some Henny and about to roll up, you smoke right?" Franklin asked.

"Occasionally," Danielle answered. "So I will take a hit or two," she said chuckling.

"Let's go to my place. It's getting cold out here and we can relax," Miguel said.

Miguel and Franklin got in the car with Danielle. They drove to his family's house on Hamilton Avenue between Rosa Parks Boulevard and East Eighteenth.

Miguel lived in the attic apartment Danielle and Inga had lived in before.

Danielle sat on the loveseat, while Franklin and Miguel sat at the small glass dining room table. Miguel passed her the blunt. She took two pulls and started coughing, and it felt as if she was coughing up her lungs. Danielle wasn't much of a smoker, so two pulls usually got her as high as she wanted to be.

Danielle, Franklin and Miguel engaged in conversation for about an hour before Franklin's girlfriend arrived outside to pick him up. Once alone, Miguel sat next to Danielle on the loveseat. The two started making out. Miguel grabbed her by the hand and led her into his room. Danielle laid down on his bed and Miguel got on top of her. They started kissing, then Miguel lifted her dress and removed her panties. She was so wet and was so spoiled when it came to oral sex, if a man didn't do that then he wasn't worth her time. Danielle started moaning because Miguel's mouth felt so good as he sucked on her pussy. Danielle had wanted Miguel back when she first met him, but she was with Vargas and he was dealing with a chubby white girl. Then he ended up going to prison. Now she finally had him.

"Aww, Miguel," Danielle moaned.

"You ready for me to stick it in?" Miguel whispered.

Danielle nodded yes.

Miguel took off his shirt and was about to grab a condom.

"No, don't put a condom on, they make me dry and irritate me,"

"Aight, turn around, I want to hit it from the back," Miguel replied.

Danielle turned around. Miguel unzipped her dress and

pulled it down. He took his finger and rubbed her pussy to make sure she was still wet, then slid his dick in her.

Miguel's dick was a little smaller than what she was used to, so it kept slipping out. Size never mattered to Danielle; if she really liked a guy, he could make her cum regardless of his size. Danielle was able to position herself better so his dick would stop slipping out, and when he was pumping his dick in her, she made sure she gripped his dick with her pussy.

"Damn, this pussy is good," Miguel said, as he was about to cum. Soon as he felt the rush come down, he took his dick out and came on her back. He picked up his shirt, which was on the floor, and wiped his cum off her. He laid down next to Danielle and gave her a kiss and they both dozed off.

Three hours passed before Danielle woke up.

Shit, I got to get home.

Danielle removed Miguel's arm that was around her and quietly got off the bed and got dressed. As she tried to tip-toe out of his room he woke up.

"You good?" he asked.

"Yeah, I got to go. When can I see you again?"

"I'll call you, don't worry. Get home safe."

Danielle got home and couldn't stop thinking about both Pedro and Miguel. She knew now that she couldn't deal with Pedro because he had a girl, and things with Miguel were starting to progress even though she knew he was probably seeing other females.

At work, Danielle kept her distance from Pedro. She and Miguel started seeing each other more often and she enjoyed going over his house chilling with him, especially since she knew his family.

Five months passed. Danielle was still involved with Miguel, however they didn't see each other as much as they used to which was starting to annoy her, and she was also getting tired of living at her aunt's house. One day out of the blue, she got a call from Ace who was now living with Bianca in an apartment on Courtland Street in Paterson, near St. Joseph hospital.

"Yo, Danielle, what's up? How is my niece?" Ace said on the other end of the phone.

"We are good, what's up with you? I heard you finally left Michelle for Bianca."

"Yo, you know me, I'm good. Yeah, I was tired of her lies, man. She is a straight hoe." Meanwhile, he was sleeping with them both and sneaking Bianca into Michelle's apartment. However, Danielle stayed out of their business.

"Bianca and I have an extra bedroom in our new apartment. You're welcome to move in and go half on the rent with us."

"How much is the rent?"

"It's eight hundred dollars, so you will pay four hundred dollars. It's a nice size apartment in a quiet neighborhood. We got a living room, a full bath and a big kitchen."

"Alright, let me come by and look at it first. Then we can talk."

Two days later, Danielle went to see Ace and Bianca. The apartment was on the first floor and it had one bedroom near the entrance, which was Ace and Bianca's room. Next to their room was the kitchen, and the bathroom sat off on the side and was a nice size. After you passed the kitchen, the living room was on the left side. On the right side was the extra bedroom they had available for Danielle and Naja. It was a big room with two windows that gave her the view of the apartments next door and it had a nice size closet.

"Oh, this is a nice size room, yes, I'll definitely take it. I can move in this Sunday. I'll give you four hundred dollars then."

"Aight, cool. I just want to make sure we all get along. I know you and Bianca had an issue last time y'all lived together. So are y'all okay with living with each other again?"

"Sure, as long as she doesn't bring that drama with her friends here," Danielle answered.

"Girl, bye. Selena and I are not even friends anymore. If I'm not hanging with my mom or kids, I'm with Ace."

"Then we cool on my end."

"Same here," Bianca replied.

That Sunday, Danielle moved in with Ace and Bianca. She found a school for Naja a few blocks away, but the only inconvenience was the longer commute to work. Instead of taking fifteen minutes to get to work, it now took her about an hour.

At work, Danielle and Pedro started speaking more especially since Danielle was getting tired of Miguel and his inconsistency. One night, Miguel called Danielle around 11:30 PM and told her to come over. Danielle told him she would be there as soon she could get a cab. After an hour, a cab finally became available to pick her up. When Danielle got to Miguel's house, she called him to say she was outside. No answer. Danielle waited a minute and called him back-to-back three times and texted him. Still no answer. Danielle was livid. *If he was going to sleep, why didn't he tell her not to come.* Danielle had to call another cab to come pick her up and take her back home.

The next day Miguel called her while she was at work.

"Yo, I told you to come by, but you took too long. I fell asleep."

"Whatever, you could've called and told me you wanted to go to sleep instead of me wasting money on a cab."

"I just dozed off, my bad."

"I got to go back to work. I'll call you later."

Danielle loved Miguel's gorgeous looks, but she couldn't tolerate the bullshit regardless of how fine he was.

It was now April 2007. Ace and Bianca broke up and Ace didn't want to lose his security deposit on the apartment, so he decided to leave the apartment to Bianca and Danielle while he moved back in with Michelle.

Danielle and Michelle's relationship was strained since Danielle became cool with Bianca. Danielle understood, but at the same time, Ace was the one cheating on her, and she kept allowing him in and out of her life. Danielle thought Michelle was just stupid and couldn't waste her time on dumb bitches.

At first it was awkward between Bianca and Danielle. Instead of communicating with each other, they would call Ace when they had complaints about each other. One day, Ace called Danielle because Bianca called him and told him Danielle was going to be late with May's rent.

"I told her I wouldn't have the money until the fourth. We have until the fifth to pay before you have to pay the late fees," Danielle told Ace over the phone.

"Yo, pay the rent. I don't want to hear nobody's mouth. I'm not losing my damn security deposit because of you two."

Danielle and Ace had a love/hate relationship. They would be cool for a while, then be at each other's throat, and Danielle didn't want to get into another altercation with him.

Why is this bitch telling him everything? He left her for his baby mom, and she is still on his dick. I can't with these dumb ass girls, Danielle thought to herself.

Danielle decided to talk to Bianca when she got home from work.

When Danielle got home, she knocked on Bianca's bedroom door.

"Come in."

"We need to talk."

"Ok sure, what about?" Bianca said with an attitude.

"If we are going to be living with each other, we are going to have to learn to communicate. Ace is not my father and will not be calling me at work yelling at me about anything. He doesn't live here. If you have a problem with me, tell me. No need for you to run to him and the same will apply to me as well. We have to learn to get along and that's it. Agreed?"

"You're right. I will come to you from now on and leave him out of it."

Bianca was glad Danielle said what she said. Now she felt she could do her and not worry about anyone telling Ace her business.

The following weekend Franklin invited Bianca, who he had a crush on, and Danielle out to his uncle's bar on Market Street to watch the Oscar De La Hoya vs. Floyd Mayweather Jr., pay-per-view fight. Danielle was surprised Miguel didn't invite her to go with him. Once the three arrived, Miguel walked in with two females. Danielle didn't say anything. Ten minutes passed and Danielle saw Miguel go in the back toward the bathroom. She headed toward the back too. She wanted to see what he was going to say since he didn't invite her but brought another female and her friend.

Miguel caught sight of her when he turned around.

"Hey, what's up Dee?"

"Hey."

Danielle couldn't believe it. He just said what's up like they were casual friends. Danielle was pissed.

When Danielle got back to the table she was sitting at with Bianca and Franklin, she told them what happened and how she felt. For the remainder of the night, Danielle kept eyeing Miguel and his company as she kept chugging down Coronas and taking shots.

Once the fight was over Danielle went outside. She wanted to beat Miguel outside so she could confront him. Everyone started coming outside and Miguel finally came out.

"Miguel, who is this nappy headed bitch with you?"

"This is my friend, chill."

"Who the fuck are you calling a nappy headed bitch?" the girl yelled back.

Miguel kept walking with his hand around the girl, as he was looking back talking to Danielle.

"Danielle, chill out. What are you mad for?"

"Fuck you, you are playing me out for that ugly ass black bitch you brought here."

"Bitch, I will fuck you up!" The girl shouted back.

Danielle still had a Corona bottle in her hand. She took the bottle and threw it at the girl. The bottle hit the curb next to where the girl was walking.

Miguel continued to walk off with the girl and her friend, as the girl continued shouting.

Bianca came over to Danielle and asked her if she was okay.

After calming down, Franklin took the girls home.

Later that night, Miguel called Danielle.

"Yo, what the fuck was that?"

"What do you mean? You invited some other female and her friend to the bar, had your hand around her, and acted like you didn't know me."

"Yo, that was just a friend, but I yo, I can't deal with the drama so I can't deal with you anymore."

"Are you serious? Wow, you are fucked up!" Danielle was so pissed off she hung up on him.

Once Miguel cut it off with Danielle, she resumed her flirting with Pedro. They started having lunch again together and talking on the phone occasionally. There were three Dominican girls that Pedro was cool with and one of them, Yonaily, was friends with Pedro's girlfriend so Danielle didn't want to make it obvious she had a crush on him.

Pedro started texting Danielle to meet him outside on Sylvan Avenue at the bus stop and the two would have make out sessions. Pedro's desk was on the other side of the office, so it wasn't obvious when they were both away from their desk, especially since they would leave five to ten minutes apart. They continued that for three months.

"Danielle, what's up?" Pedro said on the other end of the phone when she picked up.

"Hey P, I was just thinking about you, what's up?"

"I had a conversation with my girl, and Yonaily is going back and telling her we seem a little too cool and my girl wants me to stay away from you. I told her I would, but she is having Yonaily watching our interactions."

"Oh, okay then. Can you at least say hello when you see me,

right?"

"No, Danielle, no communication," Pedro answered.

Danielle wasn't hurt by the fact they couldn't make out anymore. She was more bothered because her and Pedro were cool and got along great, and his friendship was what she would really miss.

Soon after they had that conversation, Pedro was fired. The gossip around the office was that he was fired for suspicion of fraud.

Bianca and Danielle had become best friends while living together; they had so much fun together whether they hung out or stayed home.

One day in the summer of 2007, Ace called the girls and said he had to talk to them. He came over later that night.

"So, the landlord said there has been a lot of activity going on around here."

"What do you mean?" Danielle asked.

"She still thinks Bianca and I are still together and that I live here, so she thinks Bianca is sneaking dudes in here and cheating on me while I am at work. I don't want to lose my security deposit so I'm not telling her I don't live here anymore, but I am going to need y'all two to move out and I'm going to let my cousin and his girl stay here."

Danielle couldn't believe Ace was kicking them out, but she wasn't beat to argue with him. Danielle had to scramble and find an apartment.

The only person Danielle could think about that might be able to help her find an apartment was Carlos, Miguel's brother. Danielle walked over to Hamilton Avenue and spoke with Carlos. Just so happen that they were renting out the first floor apartment of their house. It was a three-bedroom apartment for eleven hundred dollars. Bianca and Danielle decided to take the apartment. Thankfully, Miguel had just moved out and was living with his new girlfriend. Danielle just hated the fact she was now living in the fourth ward. The fourth, as it was called, was not the best section of Paterson to live in.

In September, Citibank had laid off a few employees and Danielle was one of them. She decided to stay home and relax while she collected unemployment. Soon after, Vargas popped back on Danielle's radar. Flex told Vargas that Danielle was living in a three-bedroom apartment and Vargas needed a place to stay. Bianca and Danielle agreed to let him rent out the back bedroom for three hundred dollars a month. Danielle's only rule was that he wasn't allowed to bring females over.

The two were co-parenting and living under the same room with no issues. It had been three months since Vargas moved in. One night while Danielle was in his room, he walked up while talking and sipping on some Hennessy and the two started kissing. He put his hand down her panties and fingered her while tonguing her. Danielle started to get wet. Vargas started getting hard. Vargas pushed Danielle down on the bed and started to suck on her pussy. Vargas then came up and started sucking on her breast as he prepared to put his dick inside of her. Danielle continued to moan as his dick entered her. Shortly after, Danielle had an orgasm, and then another. Then she had what she felt was an ultimate orgasm as her legs began to shake uncontrollably. She was done but she didn't want to be selfish, so she allowed him to continue pumping until he came. Soon as Vargas came, he got on his back and put his legs up in the position when a woman gives birth and started to finger his own ass. Danielle looked at him like he was crazy.

"What the fuck are you doing?"

"What do you mean? I thought you liked that!"

"When did I ever say I liked that?"

"I want you to do it."

Danielle started to finger his asshole, but it felt weird.

"This is turning me off," Danielle said, as she removed her finger from his asshole. "I got to go take a shower," Danielle said, as she got up and headed out the room feeling disgusted.

In the meantime, Bianca found her a new man, an older guy from Park Avenue named Dave. Dave was twenty years her senior and Puerto Rican with hazel eyes. He wasn't bad looking for his age and he took care of Bianca. Therefore Bianca decided to move out and live with Dave on the other side of town near the Fairlawn border.

Danielle and Vargas now had the apartment to themselves. Despite their recent sexual encounter, Danielle thought maybe this time was their time because they got along so much better. However, the bliss didn't last long. Two months after they started to rekindle their relationship, Vargas started going out, not coming home at night, and stopped spending time with Danielle and Naja.

One night while Danielle and Naja were sleeping in their room, Danielle heard Vargas come in. But she also heard another voice; it was a female. Danielle just listened at first to hear what was going on. She then heard Vargas's bedroom door close and the door lock. Then she heard the girl's shoes drop to the floor. Danielle hopped out of her bed, went into the kitchen, and grabbed a knife out of the drawer so she could open Vargas's bedroom door. When she got the door open, she saw the girl with her legs wide open and Vargas eating her out.

"What the fuck are you doing?" she screamed.

The girl and Vargas were caught off guard.

"Bitch, you need to get the fuck out my house right now," Danielle shouted.

Vargas stood up and the female pulled up her pants.

"I'm confused. He told me he lived with his baby mother, but that y'all weren't together. I'm not even from around here, I'm from Newark."

Vargas stood in silence; he knew he was fucked.

"I don't give a fuck what he told you, you need to leave now!"

Danielle walked to her front door, opened it, and stood by it as the girl walked out and slammed the door.

"You dirty ass motherfucker, how dare you disrespect me! You told me we were working on getting back together, then you bring some bitch you don't even know into my house and eat her out."

"Babe, I'm so sorry. I was high as hell. Yo, I didn't mean to disrespect you. You're the only one helping me out. I love you."

"Get the fuck out of my face, all you do is lie. You're a pointless ass motherfucker."

"Babe, I'm sorry, I'll make it up to you I promise."

Vargas tried to give Danielle a kiss.

"I'm not kissing you after you just had your mouth on that bitch's pussy."

Danielle was so upset, she walked out his room and cried herself to sleep.

The first two weeks after the incident, Vargas tried to make things with Danielle good again. He knew she might kick him out anytime and he already wasn't paying her the three hundred dollars. Danielle had allowed him to slack on payments because she thought they were working on being a family. After he felt confident enough that all was good between the two, he started going back out and not coming home.

Danielle was finally over it after all these years. In the following weeks Vargas did his usual and didn't come home for days, so Danielle went into his room and took his ID and social security card. Another three days passed and still no sign of Vargas. Finally, after another five days passed, Danielle was in her room laying down when she heard Vargas and someone else come in and walked back and forth a couple of times before leaving. Danielle came out of her room and saw that Vargas had taken all of his belongings. That was the final straw. All she wanted from him was her money.

It wasn't until Vargas got a job two months later that he realized his ID and social security card were missing. He called her asking if she had seen them.

"I have them, and you won't be getting them until I get my money."

"Danielle, my boss needs them, and he won't release my check until he sees my social security card."

"Well, that's not my problem," she said, and hung up.

Two days later, Vargas called again.

"Danielle, I need my ID so I can cash my check."

"You called the other day and said you weren't getting your check because you didn't have your social. Now you have your check and need your ID to cash your check. Boy bye. Bring me my money and you can have your stuff."

Vargas was trying to say whatever he had to in order to get his stuff. However, he could tell by the way Danielle was talking she was over his bullshit and lies.

"I'll be over there tomorrow afternoon and I'll drop off the money," Vargas said, then hung up.

Danielle met Vargas outside. As he gave her the three hundred dollars, and she handed over his ID and social security card.

That was finally the end of Danielle and Vargas. Danielle felt as if the world was lifted off her shoulders.

Chapter 6

One morning, not long after she and Vargas permanently ended their relationship, she went on Myspace and looked up Pedro's profile and sent him a message. A few days later, Pedro replied and the two rekindled their friendship and would message each other occasionally. Pedro gave her the nickname "Herb," because he said she was like a little green plant with a lot of flavor.

Pedro had given her his number, but she never used it. As she sat in the house one day bored, she sent him a text.

What's up P? It's Danielle.

Hey Herb, I'm chilling at my cousin's house in Harlem. What's going on with you?

Danielle told him, her and her baby daddy were over and that she was not working now. The two texted back and forth the rest of the night.

The next morning, Pedro called her and asked if she wanted

to come hang with him in Harlem. Danielle had to drop Naja off at school, which was up the street, then she said she would be on her way.

After taking the dollar van and the A train to 145th street, she called Pedro to see where he was, and then saw him walk toward her. He was wearing a yellow shirt, army fatigue cargo shorts and the yellow and black Jordan's AJ 1. Danielle started to feel nervous the closer he got. She was really feeling him until he cut the communication between them, and here he was back in her life.

Pedro hugged her once they were face to face.

"You smoke, right?" he asked.

"A little," she replied.

"Aight cool. I got a blunt we can smoke and talk and whatever," he said.

They walked another two blocks and entered a building. They walked up three steps and entered his cousin's apartment. It was a small, but cute sized studio. There was a kitchen, a kitchen table and then a sofa, which was a pull-out bed. Danielle sat at the kitchen table while Pedro sat on the sofa and rolled the blunt. The two smoked and caught up on life. After an hour of talking the two got quiet.

"Why don't you come over and sit next to me," Pedro said.

Danielle was high and just wanted to go to sleep. However, she moved closer to Pedro. Once she sat next to him, he started to kiss her. Danielle wasn't in the mood, but she kissed him back.

While they were kissing, he started to undress her. He then leaned her back onto the sofa and pulled down his pants and told her to take off her panties.

Pedro tried to insert his dick in her, but she was dry as the Sahara. He tried kissing her neck, kissing her breast, and even ate her out, but still nothing.

"I'm sorry, I can't do this," she apologized.

"It's okay, I'm going to have blue balls, but I'll be alright," Pedro said.

Danielle could hear the aggravation in his voice even though he tried to play it off.

Danielle took that as her signal to leave.

They both got dressed and Pedro walked her to the subway and hugged her goodbye.

"I'll call you later," he said, as she walked down the stairs to the train station.

Danielle didn't hear from Pedro for a week. She thought he was turned off because he couldn't get her wet. She took it as a loss and went about her life. Another week passed and one afternoon her phone rang.

"Hello?"

"Hey D, its P."

"Oh, hey what's up? I hadn't heard from you and I thought I had turned you off."

"Nah, I got caught up in some things, but regarding that, shit happens, we can always try again if you want," Pedro said with a chuckle.

"I guess we can. Just give me some time."

"Say no more, I got you," Pedro replied.

The two talked on the phone for thirty minutes before Danielle told him she had to go run errands.

"Come by next week. I'll be at my place in the Bronx, if you want."

"That sounds like a plan, I'll hit you up for your address on Sunday night and I'll head over on Monday."

The two hung up. Danielle was happy that Pedro hadn't held their encounter against her and was looking forward to seeing him the following week.

Danielle got caught up in doing things for Naja because she was graduating from kindergarten. She didn't hit up Pedro and ignored his calls and texts. Danielle wanted to wait until the end of June after Naja's graduation, because her mom would be picking up Naja and taking her down south for the summer.

The day after Naja left, Danielle texted Pedro.

I'm sorry for not answering your call and text. I was caught up with my daughter's graduation and her leaving for the summer. Maybe I can come by tomorrow if you're free?

Two hours later Pedro responded:

I thought you got back with your baby daddy, lol. I understand, and yeah sure, tomorrow is fine. Come by early so we have more time to hang out.

How do I get there?

Once you get to 178th street, wait for the BX 11 or BX 13. Soon as the bus gets off the 181st street bridge ring the bell and you get off, it's the first stop on Ogden Avenue. I'll meet you at the bus stop, just hit me soon as you get on the bus.

Ok cool, I'll leave out around 9 AM, see you tomorrow.

The next morning Danielle headed to see Pedro. She called him once she got on the BX 11.

He said he would stop the bus just in case she didn't know what stop to get off at.

When she got off the bus Pedro gave her a peck on the lips, and she followed him across the street into his building. He lived on the first floor; his door was the last one on the left. Once he opened the green door to his apartment, you could easily tell you entered a Dominican household. The living room was colorful and very well decorated. Danielle asked to use the bathroom so she could wash her hands. This is something she had started doing faithfully when coming from outside. Pedro showed her the bathroom. After she washed her hands, she put her hands in her pants to make sure her pussy smelled good, which of course it did. She washed her hands again and returned to the living room. Pedro asked if she wanted something to drink before he rolled up. Danielle just wanted a cup of cold water.

Pedro rolled up a blunt and opened the living room window. The two sat on the fire escape. Danielle didn't want to get too high, so she took her usual two pulls and told him she was done.

They engaged in small talk until Pedro finished half the blunt and they headed back inside.

Danielle was high but she knew what was about to come next and she was hoping she could get wet this time so Pedro could get in.

They headed to his room to relax. They laid down and Danielle immediately started to undress and got under the covers.

Danielle hated when she knew she was about to have sex. She liked sex to be spontaneous, so it was up to him to get her in the mood.

Pedro laid down next to her and she laid her head on his chest and closed her eyes. Shortly after, she started moaning. Pedro started playing with her pussy with his hand; his fingers rubbing against her clit felt so good. She opened her eyes and started kissing him as she moved his hand and got on top of him. As they continued kissing, she started to rub against his dick with her pussy back and forth a few times, then she was ready for him to slide in. As he started to kiss on her neck, she stopped him, then turned around and got in the backward cowgirl position.

Pedro liked the way she took control. He sat up and placed his hand on her breast as she rode his dick, throwing her ass back. Pedro was turned on and he lifted himself a little so his dick could go in more. Danielle then hopped off his dick and laid down so he could do missionary and so that she could cum. Danielle grabbed his dick with her pussy and grinded on it until she came. Pedro had already came since he was a minute man, but he wanted to make sure she was sexually satisfied. Danielle let out a big, long moan and started to breathe heavy. She was done. Pedro got off from on top of her and laid down next to her; they both knocked out.

After waking up two hours later, Danielle asked if she could take a shower. She then got dressed and Pedro walked her to the bus stop. When the BX 11 arrived, they kissed each other goodbye and she headed back to New Jersey. Pedro really started to like Danielle and she felt the same way. Everything between the two was great. They traveled together, went out to eat and spent just about every day with each other. They even started a Nutcracker (A vodka and rum drink with fruit punch) and weed business together. Danielle loved the idea of her and her man working and making money together.

Chapter 7

After being together for two and a half years, the two were hanging out at Danielle's new apartment in her hometown of Teaneck, which was a block away from Votee Park, the local park the town is known for. Danielle hopped in her 1999 red Honda Accord to take him back to the Bronx. While in the car, Danielle put on Trey Songz CD *Ready* and played track number five, "One Love."

"I want you to listen to this song," she said, "this is how I feel about you."

Pedro listened as the song played.

Danielle sang along to the chorus:

"'You are all I need and I'll never let go'
You are all I need and I'll never let go

(Never let go of you)

And here I am (here I am)
I'm your man (I'm your man)
I came with everything you needed
You and me undefeated,
Till the end of time
One mind, one heart, one love
All you gotta do is,
Take my hand (take my hand)
We will stand (we will stand)
This was made to last forever,
So let's say it together for the rest of time
One mind, one heart, one love."

"I never heard that song, I like it babe," Pedro said, as the song went off.

Danielle arrived at Pedro's house and as he got out, he kissed her goodbye.

Danielle put the song on repeat while heading back to Jersey.

Danielle thought she was in love and had found the one. Pedro had told her one day when they had taken a trip to VA Beach, that he would only get married if a female got pregnant by him or made him cum while sucking his dick. Danielle didn't want another kid, but she started watching porn and YouTube videos on how to make a man cum while giving head.

Danielle thought everything between the two would only get better. Especially because she hadn't been with someone so long consecutively.

The following week she went to his house and he asked her if she could help him clean up and do the dishes.

"You had a party?"

"Nah, my brother had a few friends over last night."

Well damn, why didn't he invite me? Danielle thought. She knew his brother and they were cool.

"Oh, okay," Danielle replied.

It kept bothering Danielle that he hadn't invited her over, so when she returned home that evening, she went to Pedro's Facebook page to see if anyone tagged or posted a picture of him from his brother's party.

When she went to his page and saw just that. A girl by the name of Fran had posted a picture of her and Pedro together outside of his apartment from that night, and she had his hat on her head.

Danielle read the comments under the picture. It was the girl, her friend and Pedro commenting. In one of the comments, Fran said something in reference to his worm.

Danielle wondered if the girl was referring to his dick as being a worm.

Everything was going so good between the two and now she felt as if everything wasn't as wonderful as she thought.

Two days later, Pedro came over her house again and they fucked. He wanted her to give him head but she wasn't in the mood, especially since she wanted to get down to figuring out the truth behind the Fran situation.

He went to go take a shower and left his phone on her dresser. She took it and went through his texts. She saw Fran's name and went to the messages. She scrolled quickly through them.

Danielle stopped in disbelief when saw:

Pedro: *"I thought of you when I heard this:* **Take my hand (take my hand)**
We will stand (we will stand)
This was made to last forever,
So let's say it together for the rest of time
One mind, one heart, one love."

Fran replied with heart emojis.

Danielle felt her heart drop. She just told him that song was the song she associated with him, and here he was texting the lyrics to another female. Danielle was crushed.

She put the phone back on the dresser and laid back down. She was pissed but didn't want Pedro to suspect her of creeping through his phone.

As she dropped him back home, he felt her energy was off, but she told him everything was ok.

After he exited the car, Danielle felt a teardrop roll down her face when thinking about how she felt when she saw he sent another female those lyrics.

"Mrs. Davis, don't forget you have a meeting at 11:30 AM with a new sponsor, and you have lunch with your lawyer at 1:30 PM," Danielle's assistant Tanisha buzzed through the phone intercom.

Danielle loved when she heard someone calling her Mrs. Davis. She looked at her ring and her tears of sadness turned to tears of happiness. Danielle wiped the tear from her eye and took a big gulp.

"Thanks Tanisha. By the way, I need you to hold my calls unless it is Stefan or any of my children. Oh, Tanisha, you can leave for the day after I return from my meeting."

"Sure, and thanks, Mrs. Davis," Tanisha said, as she smiled through the intercom.

Tanisha was five-six, 190 pounds, with brown skin, long black hair and in her mid-thirties. She was also once a struggling, single mom with her ten-year-old daughter. Danielle loved her energy during her interview and could relate to her. She hired her on the spot six months ago, after she had to fire her other assistant Karla for not completing assignments and being constantly on the phone with her boyfriend all day.

Tanisha had so much respect for Danielle. Tanisha loved how a single mom of four worked hard and became successful with her career and with love. Danielle was an inspiration for her.

Danielle put her finger on her wedding band and twisted it as she thought of Stefan. He was such a blessing; he was her definition of perfection for a man. Another tear rolled down her cheek as she thought about how much she loved him.

Danielle thought back to when things came to an end with Pedro. After seeing the texts between Pedro and Fran, a week had passed before she went over his house and confronted him.

"What's up D, you have been acting weird lately, is everything ok?"

"Well actually, no it's not. I went through your phone last week when you came over and saw that you had texted some girl named Fran the lyrics to "One Love." I told you that song was how I felt about you, and you go and text it to another female? Are you fucking serious?"

"Well first of all, why were you in my phone? That means I can't trust you, and if you must know, I only sent her that because she is into music and I thought she would like that song."

Danielle could see how he was trying to do reverse psychology with the *I can't trust you, bullshit.*

"She is into music, oh okay."

That was the best he could do? Danielle thought.

That didn't even sound plausible, but she wasn't one who was into arguing; so she went along with his story. However, she started to pay more attention to his movements.

Danielle wanted to spice things up a little. So the following day after she took her car to the shop, she went home, took off all her clothes and just put on a black trench coat she had. She hopped on the 178 bus and took it to the George Washington Bridge Terminal and hopped on the BX 11.

She buzzed Pedro's bell. After he buzzed her in, she heard the door to his apartment opening. Once she saw him open the door, she opened her coat.

"You came all the way over here on the bus with no clothes on? It's October," he said, as he shook his head. "You're crazy! But get your ass in here."

Soon as she stepped in, she dropped her coat to the floor.

"I need you to sit down," she instructed him.

Pedro sat down on the green, leather love seat.

Danielle loosened his belt and tugged down his pants.

She took out his dick and started stroking it with her hand while spitting on it. Danielle then sucked his dick going up and down. Soon his dick got harder and bigger and she knew it was time to get on top. She sat on him facing him and inserted his dick into her and started to ride him going up and down while he sucked on her breast, which made her wet. Pedro then lifted

97

her up, carried her into the bedroom, threw her on the bed and started fucking her missionary until he nutted. Pedro loved how her pussy was fat and tight.

After he came, he laid his head on her chest as she dozed off. Pedro started feeling guilty for messing around with Fran. They hadn't had sex, but he did make out with her a few times and she did suck him off that night after his brother's party. Pedro cared about Danielle, but he felt they needed space. They were always together. He wanted to miss her.

Danielle started to feel like she could no longer trust Pedro. She was starting to feel like she did when she was with Vargas. She knew she was being deceived, but just not to the same extreme.

Six months went by and everything seemed to be back to normal. Pedro, who was getting unemployment, got a job at his cousin's club as the club manager, but it was in Jamaica, Queens. His cousin also gave him an apartment above the club. Danielle was happy he got a job, but now he was going to be farther away. Danielle's car was still in the shop. So in order to see Pedro, she would have to take a bus to Port Authority in New York City, then hop on the E train and take it to the last stop and walk to Jamaica Avenue and get a taxi to his apartment. The trip took a total of two hours.

Pedro had a small one-bedroom apartment. He barely had any furniture in it and was sleeping on an airbed. His new apartment didn't feel as cozy as his mom's apartment in the Bronx and now that he moved, he seemed to rush her out when she came over.

One night, Danielle was at a club in Manhattan with her best guy friend Juan. As they were leaving, she called Pedro and told him she was coming over, which he agreed to. She was drunk as hell but managed to get to her destination.

Pedro met her downstairs at the club since he was closing. Pedro ended up fucking her doggy style on the black benches in the club before heading upstairs to his apartment. When they got upstairs, Danielle passed out on his air mattress.

"Hey sleepy head," Pedro said, as she woke the next morning.

"What time is it?" she asked.

"Around 11 AM."

"Damn, I was drunk as hell," Danielle said laughing.

"Yeah, you were, but umm, what time you plan on leaving?"

Danielle looked at him puzzled; now that he had his own place he acted as if he didn't want her hanging around longer then she needed to.

"Well, I'll get ready to go now."

"I'm not rushing you; I was just asking."

Danielle wasn't buying it; something seemed off.

Chapter 8

It was New Year's Eve and Danielle made her 2010 new year's resolution to get a full-time job and save her money. Danielle and Naja had moved from their apartment in Teaneck and shared an apartment with Bianca once again. Dave had gotten locked up and was sentenced to four years. He left Bianca the two-bedroom apartment they shared which was on East Thirty-Eighth Street. The apartment was modern and up to date and Bianca loved interior designing, so the apartment was beautifully furnished.

Now that Danielle was even farther from Pedro, they saw less and less of each other, but would call and text each other daily. One night after asking Bianca to watch Naja, she drove to go see Pedro. Pedro had since gotten a bed, and after they had sex, the two stayed up late to talk. Danielle wanted to see where they stood.

"P, do you love me?"

"Danielle, really?"

"Yes really. I want to know, and I want an honest answer."

There was silence for a minute.

"I have love for you, and I do care about you a lot, but I'm not in love with you."

Danielle felt hurt but didn't show it.

How are you with someone for three years and you're not in love with them? Danielle thought. He was basically wasting her time. They had only broken up a few days at the most but were basically together the entire three years. All that time, and he still wasn't in love with her.

That was when Danielle realized the relationship wasn't going anywhere, especially with them seeing less and less of each other. He was working in a club and she didn't know if he was seeing someone else out there. The energy between them seemed off. They weren't heading in the same direction anymore.

"Oh, okay. That's cool," Danielle replied.

Pedro wrapped his arm around her and gave her a kiss to make her feel better. He sensed she was not happy with that answer. They both dozed off until the next morning.

They continued their distant relationship. They were six months away from their four-year anniversary. Danielle couldn't get the words, *"I have love for you, but I'm not in love with you,"* out of her head. She thought she was in love with him but couldn't continue to be with someone who wasn't in love with her.

In the meantime, Danielle got a job at a doctor's office in Englewood on Grand Avenue near Route Four. The pay was good and her co-workers seemed nice. However, the office manager wasn't as friendly, so Danielle stayed out of her way.

It was now March. Danielle had been at her job for a month

and hadn't seen Pedro since the first week of February, the week before she got hired. It was a Friday night, and she was horny, so she called him up.

"Hey babe, what's up?" Pedro answered, when he picked up the phone.

"Hey, I miss you, I wanted to come over."

"I miss you too. I'll be closing up the club in an hour, so you can come by then."

Danielle needed Bianca to watch Naja, so she knocked on Bianca's door, who was in her bedroom with Jose, Vargas's friend, who she was now seeing.

"I'm heading out to Queens to see P. Just listen out for Naja if she wakes up."

"Ok, D, I got you. Be safe driving to Queens this late."

"Thanks, bestie," Danielle said, as she headed out. After driving to Queens, the two had sex. However, this sex was different. It didn't feel right. It was like neither of them had put any emotion into it. It felt like a quick nut. Danielle woke up early the next morning; Pedro was still asleep. She got up and quickly got dressed and gathered her things.

"You leaving?" Pedro said, after he was awakened by her movement.

"Yeah, imma head out. I got to get back to Naja."

Pedro knew something was wrong. It was never like Danielle to get up and leave. She gave him a peck on the lips before she left out the front door. A few days later Pedro called her, but she didn't answer. He called again the next day and still no answer. They both sensed it was the end of the relationship, but Pedro felt bad because he in fact had started a new relationship with someone else and didn't want to hurt Danielle's feelings. Danielle helped him when he wasn't working and had no money. They had fun together and he did care about her, but the distance had put a strain on what could've been. Pedro knew Danielle felt a shift in their relationship. Especially because Danielle never went a day without calling or texting him, and if he called and she missed the call, she would call back within a few hours.

Pedro then sent her a text:

Danielle, you will always hold a special place with me, so don't act like I'm gone forever, aight. Sorry about what I did and didn't do, and hopefully we could just move on and still be cool. No grudges muahzzzz. At the end of the day, you were the moon that lit my night up.

Danielle read the text; she blushed a little, but never responded. That was the last time she heard from him.

Chapter 9

It was now 2012 and Instagram was becoming the new go-to social media site and Danielle got a friend request from this handsome chocolate brother. Danielle was never a fan of Black guys, especially ones that were darker than her, but Stefan caught her attention for some reason. They had mutual followers, so she accepted him and discovered he was from the neighboring town. He was six years her senior and tall with a nice frame. You could tell he worked out. Not only was he handsome, but by his pictures she could tell he was a mature MAN. He had a house, drove a Mercedes C Class and dressed well.

Shortly after friending Stefan on Instagram, a local party promoter, Donny F, was throwing a party at *FEEL GOOD LOUNGE* in Secaucus, New Jersey. Danielle made plans to go with her younger cousin Toya. Toya was seven years younger than Danielle, but they grew close as they got older. Toya was about five foot tall, light skinned with a pretty face, and had a big butt and long hair that came down to her waist. She was half Black and half Puerto Rican. All the boys gave Toya their full attention because of her beautiful looks.

Danielle didn't expect to see anyone that she hadn't seen before. Once they arrived, they headed straight to the bar. As Danielle was ordering drinks, she looked to her left and saw Stefan and he was with two of his friends. Danielle had met one of the guys Stefan was with a few months back. Everyone called him Freeze. Danielle met Freeze at a clothing store in Paterson that he was opening with Danielle's friend Alisa's boyfriend, Simon, as well as two other guys named Mike and Lamar.

Danielle's heart started beating fast; almost as if she was having an anxiety attack. She couldn't believe she was seeing Stefan in person and didn't know what to say, or if she should say anything. Danielle never approached a guy, she always let a guy approach her, but something about Stefan was different. Toya was being entertained by some guys at the bar. Danielle tapped her on the shoulder.

"Hey, you see those three dudes at the end of the bar?"

"Yeah, what about them?"

"Do you know them?" Danielle asked.

"They are some older guys from my town, but I don't know them."

"Oh, well the one in the middle is my friend on Instagram, and I think he is so fine."

"Uh, but he is Black. Since when do you like Black dudes?"

"Yeah, I know, there is just something about him!" Danielle said while blushing. "I'm going to go say hi."

105

Toya chuckled as Danielle walked over to Stefan nervously, not believing she was going to talk to him.

As she walked up to him, she took a deep breath, "Hey."

Stefan looked at her casually and said, "What's up?"

Danielle's heart started racing, *what can I say now?* she thought to herself.

"Aren't we friends on Instagram?"

"Yeah, we are." Stefan said nonchalantly.

Danielle started to feel regret and disappointment flow hot in her veins. "Well, I just wanted to come over and say hi."

"Yeah ok, well I'm about to head into the party. I'll see you around."

Danielle turned around and walked back to the bar where Toya was standing there waiting for her. Soon as she approached Toya, Danielle saw Stefan and his friends walk past and enter the dance floor of the lounge. Danielle felt like a fool. It took all of her courage to go up and try to have a conversation with her Instagram crush who seemed entirely uninterested in her. *I'm such a fool. I shouldn't have gone up to him, he is out of my league. I must not be pretty enough for him.* She thought to herself.

She and Toya entered the dance floor as well. They had guys buy them drinks while they joked on some of the outfits that other girls wore. The whole night while catching laughs and throwing back drinks with Toya, Danielle kept trying to catch a glimpse of Stefan, but after she realized she couldn't keep up with his every move she let her thoughts of him go.

Danielle didn't know how to feel about Stefan since he shrugged her off at the party a few months back, but he was still liking her pictures on Instagram. She figured she may still have a shot. Donny F's last party was five months ago, and Toya heard he was throwing another one.

"Girl, Donny F is throwing another party but this time it's at SoHo Lounge in Fort Lee. Are you going?" Toya asked Danielle on the other end of the phone.

"I was thinking about it, but I always see local faces. But if I go, you're going with me."

"Oh man, I want to go but I have to head back to Maryland, classes start next week." Toya was in her senior year at Morgan State University, so she wasn't around as much as Danielle wished.

That following weekend was the party. Danielle decided to go to the party by herself, just to get out of the house.

Danielle had moved out of Paterson and got a studio apartment in Englewood, New Jersey. She barely had a sitter for her ten-year-old daughter Naja, so she often left her alone in their apartment with the TV being her sitter. Unable to afford to get her hair done, Danielle threw on a wig, some tight indigo color skinny jeans, a purple shirt and a denim indigo vest that matched her jeans perfectly and threw on some navy-blue suede booties she had brought from Bakers. She added some gold accessories on her neck and arm to top of her outfit.

Danielle hopped on the 178 New Jersey Transit bus that stopped a block away from her house and got off at George Washington Bridge Plaza in Fort Lee and walked a half a block to SoHo Lounge. When she entered the club, she started looking for familiar faces so she could hang with them for the night. She ran into a few people from town and stopped and chatted before heading to the bar for a drink. She ordered her usual go-to drink, Vodka and Cranberry. As she was drinking, she started checking out all who were there. A lot of faces she knew; some from school and some from seeing around town. She ran into one of her older cousins' friends named Tammy, who was talking to her near the DJ and VIP area where Donny F was hanging out at. As Danielle was talking to Tammy, Mike, who Danielle had met at the clothing store some months back with Alisa, was waving for Danielle to come see him in VIP. Security let her in and she sat next to Mike.

"What's up, woman?"

"Nothing much, just wanted to come out for a minute."

"Who you here with?" he asked looking around.

"Nobody, just me."

"Well, stay here and drink with me."

Mike had a bottle of Monet and poured Danielle a glass. Mike was that guy. Everyone knew him. He was known as a get money nigga around town. When out, he liked to be seen and flashed his money. He was always in VIP and he didn't mind spending money because he always had money coming in. He wore a big, gaudy diamond ring on his pinky finger that reminded Danielle of her father who also wore big diamond rings on his pinky.

Danielle though Mike was nice, and he was handsome, but he wasn't her type. He was six-two, 215 pounds, dark skinned, had nice almond eyes with a big beautiful sexy smile. Simon and Alisha tried to hook them up that day at the clothing store. Simon had given Mike Danielle's number. The two had spoken on the phone briefly but no sparks flew, and Danielle wasn't interested in him in that way.

Danielle hung with Mike the rest of the night. They drank only the best top-shelf liquor, laughed and watched everyone floating in and out of the VIP section.

As the night came to an end, Danielle realized she needed a ride home and the buses weren't running at 2 AM. Danielle asked Mike if he could get her a ride home.

"Sure, I can get you a ride but let's go to Route 4 Diner for breakfast."

"Ok, sure," Danielle replied, as she gathered her things to leave.

The two hopped in a car with Mike's friends and got dropped off at the diner for breakfast.

"Yo, order whatever you want it's on me," Mike said to Danielle, who was looking at the menu.

Danielle didn't want him to think she was going to take advantage of him just because he told her to get whatever she wanted, so she ordered a simple breakfast: sausage, toast and corn beef hash. When it was time to pay Mike whipped out a knot full of money. For some reason, Danielle felt Mike was showing off when he pulled all that money out of his pocket. She was instantly turned off by that. Mike got Danielle home safe and sound. She went in her apartment and fell out next to Naja who was fast asleep in the bed they shared.

Chapter 10

Ayear and a half had passed, and it was now the summer of 2013 and Danielle, who was now in her early thirties, was working part-time at Simply Seafood on Palisades Avenue in Englewood. The restaurant was owned by Leland Robinson, the son of Sylvia Robinson, who had owned Sugar Hill Records and was known for her song "Pillow Talk," in the late 70s. Danielle worked there a few days out of the week for extra money outside of her job at the doctor's office.

"Hey, I didn't know you worked here," Stefan said, when he walked in to order and saw Danielle at the counter.

Danielle's heart jumped. "Hey, what's up? Yeah, this is my part-time job," Danielle answered bashfully.

"Nothing wrong with that. I just came by to order the seafood combo platter."

It had been two years since she last saw Stefan at Donny F's party. They hadn't communicated with each other aside from liking each other photos on Instagram. Danielle turned around to give the cook Stefan's order. She was so nervous. She never had an anxiety attack but whenever she got around him, she felt as if she was having one with the way he made her feel.

"I know I was kind of rude to you when I saw you last, so let me get your number, so I can take you out and make up for it," Stefan said.

Danielle wanted to kick herself; she was so mad that he said that to her now.

Just two days prior, Danielle found out she was pregnant by the guy she had been fucking for the last year. She didn't like the guy like that, it was just sex and he kept her company despite the fact he had a girlfriend of twelve years that Danielle recently found out about. At that moment Danielle wished she wasn't pregnant. The guy she really wanted was asking her out, and she was newly pregnant by a guy she was fucking for company.

Danielle took a deep breath. "I would give you my number, but I'm pregnant," she said with disappointment.

Stefan looked just as disappointed when she said that.

"Alright, that's cool. Congratulations."

They both got quiet and the silence made the situation even more awkward.

Finally, his food was ready. She wrapped his food in a plastic bag and handed it to him.

"Take care," Stefan said, as he turned to leave.

"You too," she replied.

Danielle was upset with herself but there was nothing she could do about the situation. She took another deep breath, saddened about what could have been and went back to work.

Hector was Danielle's new baby daddy. She first met him at her cousin's house in Paterson. He was nice looking, not a Stefan in her eyes, but he was fuckable. He was six feet, 225 pounds, light skinned, Puerto Rican and three years her senior. He seemed nice, but outside of his looks he was not Danielle's type. He had given her a ride home to her apartment in Englewood late one night while they both were at her cousin's house, and had the nerve to charge her five dollars when he offered her a ride. That was a total turn off for her. When he reached her apartment, he asked her for her number. She was reluctant to give it to him but ended up giving it to him anyway, a decision Danielle would later come to regret.

Two days later Hector called her. The two seemed to hit it off on the phone. He told her he worked part-time as a truck driver and the rest of the time he sold cocaine. Danielle really didn't want another drug dealer in her life, but Hector told her he wanted out of that lifestyle. He wanted a family and a relationship with God.

Hector had been in a twelve-year relationship with Julia, unbeknownst to Danielle. Julia was an older black woman, ten years his senior. She worked for New Jersey Transit and had three daughters from previous relationships. They had briefly broken up for a couple of weeks and in that time, Hector met Danielle. Hector also left out important details such as he also no longer drove trucks, was a full-time drug dealer, had a rap sheet a mile long for hitting women, was addicted to PCP, and he and Julia were in the process of working on their relationship and he had moved back in to her place.

After Stefan left the restaurant, Danielle was in deep thought when her cell phone rang. She didn't recognize the number, but it was a 973 number, most likely a Paterson number, so she answered:

"Hello?"

"This is Julia, and Hector is here. Are you pregnant? And if so, are you keeping it?"

"If he is there, ask him, why are you calling me?" Danielle said pissed off. *Why the hell is this chick calling me and why is Hector over at her house?* Danielle thought.

"You stupid bitch. I've been with him twelve years and you start fucking my man and now you're pregnant. Bitch, you are nothing but a home wrecker and a groupie!" Julia yelled through the phone

Julia had searched for Danielle on Facebook and seen her pictures with DJ Self and Fred Da Godson at a bunch of different parties. She took Danielle for a groupie, trying to hop on anyone with money to fuck. However, that was far from the truth.

Danielle hung up on Julia. She wasn't about to stress herself out over this broad. Danielle wished she had saw through the lies Hector told her, but here she was pregnant, dealing with drama and lost the opportunity with the guy she really wanted.

Julia and Hector had a turbulent relationship for those twelve years, but she loved him. He cheated and she cheated. She put up with his drug addiction and his numerous domestic violence convictions, but they always worked through it. During the time Danielle was pregnant, Julia lost her job because she was with Hector when he was slinging coke to one of his customers, and the police were watching and pulled them over and locked up both Julia and Hector. Julia had been through a lot with Hector and wasn't going to let this younger female come out of nowhere and take her man, pregnant or not. She had invested too much of herself into him.

Hector loved Julia but wasn't in love with her. He didn't even love himself. He loved money and PCP, and when he was high on PCP, he then showed Julia how much he was "in love" with her. Often facetiming her, crying and telling her how much he loved her and her daughters. Hector and Julia always played a game of tit for tat. Hector would cheat, then Julia would cheat. They played this game all the time but always came back together. Hector wanted this time to be the same, but the fact that Danielle was keeping the baby and Hector continually lying to her, telling her that he and Julia were over when they weren't, just kept making the situation on all sides worse.

Julia called and texted Danielle throughout her whole pregnancy, and at one point told Danielle she hoped the baby died. When Danielle was eight months pregnant, she finally got tired of the harassment and told Hector to decide after going through his phone and finding proof that he was still living with and fucking Julia.

Hector was nothing he claimed, and Danielle felt let down. She had really let herself down, all because she was lonely and wanted to feel loved, even if it was from someone she didn't want to be with. Her baby boy was on the way any day now, and she wanted to have a family for her son even if she wasn't happy. She already let Naja down in that department and didn't want to repeat the same mistakes with her baby boy.

Danielle moved into a new apartment in Teaneck, her hometown. Danielle and Hector had agreed that he would move in after the baby was born.

On April Fool's day 2014, Danielle gave birth to a healthy nine pound, three ounce, baby boy she had decided to name Mason Lee Cruz. His face was the same as hers, but he had the pale skin color of his Puerto Rican father. Once it was time for Danielle to check out and go home, she not only had to adjust to having a newborn in her life again after almost twelve years, but she also had to adjust to living with a man, especially one she didn't see a real future with. Since the two started fucking back in 2012, Danielle acted as if she hated sucking dick. She "attempted" once with Hector but told him his dick was too big and she felt kind of repulsed by it, when in actuality she was repulsed by him. She enjoyed the power sucking dick gave her when she actually liked the person, but when she didn't like someone, she played it off like dick sucking was the most disgusting thing there was to do. Even when Hector ate her out, she felt like she was being raped by his mouth and wanted him to get off of her. The sexual rabbit she was once, she was no longer. The six weeks of no sex after birth was a relief, since she didn't have to have him wallowing on top of her, but soon that reprieve would be over, and she would have to succumb to his voracious sexual appetite.

Danielle planned to breastfeed Mason like she did Naja so that she could lose her pregnancy fat fast and get her body back into shape. However, Hector cooked for her every day, which helped her keep the weight on. Toya and her mother Monica were convinced that Hector was purposely keeping Danielle fat so that she wouldn't be appealing to anyone but him, and she would no longer want to go out and party like she did before she got pregnant.

Monica and Toya were not far off. Hector started to get

possessive over Danielle. He wouldn't let her go out. He kept her plump, and her confidence in the gutter. He laid in the bed all day and watched TV or played video games. Despite the fact her and Stefan never did anything but have a conversation which Hector never knew about; he would accuse her of fucking him because he would catch her looking at his pictures on Instagram. Danielle had to pay all the bills with her maternity leave money, as well as take care of Naja, Mason, herself and Hector with her money. Danielle was miserable, however when Alisa or anyone else came over or called they believed Danielle had that "Happy Family Life." But what looks happy on the outside, isn't always good on the inside.

What Danielle failed to notice—because she was wrapped up in all the drama with Hector—was that Naja wasn't happy. It had been just them two for so many years, and now Hector and a new baby took up Danielle's time leaving Naja feeling neglected by both her mother and father.

Instead of focusing and spending time with Naja, Danielle was going over to Michelle's house to hang out, especially since she was now dating their old friend Diablo who now lived with her.

Michelle was still upset with Danielle for picking Bianca over her and telling Bianca that Michelle had lied about miscarrying Ace's baby when she had got an abortion. However, Michelle was willing to forgive Danielle, but she just became cautious about information she shared with her. The two reconnected prior to Danielle giving birth to Mason, and Hector and Diablo knew each other from Passaic County Jail where they had been locked up together in the past.

Danielle felt like she had a good time in life; she partied, popped bottles, looked cute, but now that was all over. She had turned into a fat mother of two children and stuck with a bum whom she felt she couldn't escape from. She always wanted to get married, despite the fact she wanted a big wedding with someone she could see herself with forever, but figured her and Hector might as well get married. Plus, that was what Hector wanted and Danielle would be able give her kids a family they deserved. Danielle picked up the marriage license application from the town hall and filled her section out and gave it to Hector for him to fill out his section.

Danielle was supposed to hand in the marriage application to town hall and pay the twenty-eight dollar registration fee. However, the thought of having to be with Hector forever seemed to become more and more daunting.

Why, should I lower my standards and settle? I'm not happy. I want to make a family for my children, but Naja hates Hector and Mason is too young to realize what's going on. This fool doesn't even have money saved or a bank account and he is only making nine dollars an hour at the local Jewish Deli on the other side of town. Being unhappy for the remainder of my life just so my kids can have a father figure is not worth it. Danielle thought to herself repeatedly. Danielle helped Hector get a job, since one of the patients from her job owned a well-known Jewish Deli. She told him her boyfriend needed a job and he told her to have him come in for an interview. Hector got the job and barely wanted to give Danielle four hundred dollars a month to help pay the one thousand dollar rent, all while she continued to clothe herself and the kids, pay the light bill, car insurance, gas and the cable bill.

When she met Hector, he had a Nissan Z3. It was in Julia's

name but shortly before Danielle gave birth to Mason, Julia reported the car stolen and he had to turn it back in. Shortly after, Danielle purchased an old, rusty six hundred-dollar 1997 Nissan Altima.

How can a man live with the mother of his child and expect her to pay most of the bills, not even chipping in half of the living expenses, then have an attitude on top of that?

A few weeks passed and Hector asked her whatever happened with the marriage application and when were they going to get married. Unbeknownst to him, Danielle had ripped the paper up a few days after he filled it out.

"I changed my mind!" Danielle told him.

"What do you mean? I thought you wanted a family?"

"I do, but just not with you," Danielle finally had the courage to say.

She was tired of him and wanted him gone from her life. She really wanted him gone out of her life forever but knew that wasn't going to happen.

Hector started to feel the change in Danielle. She barely wanted to have sex with him and eventually made him sleep on the living room couch. Days turned into weeks and Hector was trying to "step up" but Danielle wasn't having it. She let him know every chance she got that he was a bum and a lazy piece of shit.

Danielle started going on social media again. She stopped logging on because Hector was calling her a groupie and accusing her of sleeping with Stefan, who she hadn't spoken to since she saw him at the restaurant and broke the news to him that she was pregnant. Danielle was ready to move on and get Hector out of her house and her life.

"I got fired today," Hector said.

"You what? How the hell did that happen?"

"This asshole tried to tell me to take a box down to the basement. Shit was heavy as hell."

"Ok, so how did you get fired?"

"Yo, Danielle, taking a box down the stairs is not my fucking job. I was hired to prepare food, not be an errand boy and carry boxes to the basement."

"Wait, wait, wait..." Danielle had to process what Hector told her. "You got fired because your boss told you to take a box down the stairs? Are you fucking kidding me? Last I checked if your boss told you to take a box to the basement, you take it."

"Fuck outta here," Hector replied with a snort.

All Danielle could do was walk out of the kitchen and go into her bedroom. She couldn't wrap her mind around how she ended up with a big ass dummy. A dude that expected her to carry all the weight and then lose a job that was barely helping anyway, all because he didn't want to take a box to the basement for his boss. That was the last straw for her. She could no longer deal with someone she knew was not on her level and so beneath her standards.

Danielle returned to the kitchen.

"I can't do this anymore; I want you out!"

"What do you mean? I'll get another job."

"No, I don't want you around anymore. I'm not happy; this just isn't working."

"You fucking someone else? I see you on Facebook and Instagram all night long. I know your fucking that @Stefanisme person on IG or whatever his damn name is," Hector said with anger clearly evident in his voice.

"I don't even know him like that, I only like his pictures," Danielle said, as she got up to exit the kitchen. But before she could reach the kitchen door, Hector swung and punched her in the face causing her to scream as she landed on the kitchen floor.

Besides Ace, Danielle had never been hit by a man she was involved with. All she could do was lay on the floor crying.

"Get the fuck up. I didn't even hit you that hard."

"What the fuck do you mean? You hit me just because you think I'm fucking someone I'm not," Danielle said with tears streaming down her face. "I want you out, and I want you out now!" Danielle screamed.

"I ain't going nowhere!" Hector yelled back, as he headed out the kitchen.

Danielle felt trapped in her own home. She didn't know how to get Hector out. She could've called the police, but she didn't want people in her business. Especially living on one of the main streets in her hometown where people she grew up with and went to school with lived. She couldn't understand why God continually punished her with no good men. All Danielle ever wanted was to find a man that was in love with her and a man she could marry, love, be submissive to and love 'til death do them part.

The doorbell rang.

"Naja, who is at the door?"

"It's Hector."

"Oh, he doesn't have his keys. Don't open that door," Danielle demanded.

Danielle's cell phone rang.

"Hello?"

"Open the fucking door."

"Where your keys at?"

"I lost them last week sometime."

"That's good to hear, I'm not letting you back in. I told you I wanted you out."

"Bitch, you better let me in!"

"I will call the cops and have them lock your ass up."

"You stupid bitch!" Hector yelled, as he kicked the door and walked off.

It had been three weeks since the incident where Hector punched her in the face and finally Danielle was able to get Hector out of her house. Every day she wished she could've called Julia and beg her to take Hector back, but the two women had come to hate each other over this bum ass guy who wasn't worth a quarter, so calling her was definitely out of the question. Danielle had fought for Hector thinking she was getting a prize, but much to her surprise he was far from any prize.

Danielle started feeling like she could finally breathe in her own home. Naja was relieved Hector was gone. She hated him. Naja thought he was lazy, bossy and not good enough for her mom. She had seen her mom cry many nights for many years. Her mom was tough on her and left her alone a lot, but her mom just wanted someone to love her. She had seen her mom do so many good things for people to always end up alone and hurt, and she couldn't figure out why her mom kept allowing people to hurt her. Naja had her own issues because she was getting older and started to resent her dad more and more, especially since he contributed to her mom's suffering by not helping them or even picking up a phone to say he wanted to see Naja or that he loved her. This was the first time she saw her mother happy someone was out of her life and instead of crying she was smiling.

Chapter 11

It had been four months since Danielle kicked Hector out. He was steady calling and texting her, calling her obscene names. Danielle thought Hector was bipolar. One minute he would call and apologize and say he wanted his family back, then soon as she got him off the phone he would call her back and say she was whore, bitch this, bitch that, and she would hang up and he would text her saying how nobody would want her. This went on almost every day for a week until Danielle finally blocked his number.

It was now April 2015. Danielle was at work when an Edible Arrangements delivery guy walked up to her desk.

"Is there a Danielle Lee here?"

"Yes, that's me."

"Well, this is for you."

It was a big basket with a bunch of beautifully decorated fruit including her favorite, chocolate covered strawberries. Danielle quickly opened the card to see who sent them. When she opened the card and saw the sender's name, her smile quickly turned into a frown. She tore the card up and threw it in the garbage and took the fruit basket and put it in the break room and told everyone there was fruit in the kitchen for anyone that wanted some. Danielle didn't even read the note written inside the card. She saw the name Hector and immediately wanted to discard the whole thing.

As she returned from the kitchen, she got a text on her cell phone.

Did you get your special delivery? Hector texted

Yup, I threw it in the garbage, Danielle texted back, right before she blocked his number again.

She just wanted Hector to leave her alone. The week before, he had come to her apartment in the middle of the night banging on the door asking her to let him in, then went to her bedroom window and tried to get in through the window with the AC. It was a failed attempt, but he put a hole through the organ part of the AC.

Danielle had a lost a few pounds since she kicked him out the house and was ready to date again, but was taking it slow because she didn't want him popping up while she had company.

Danielle was starting to feel confident once again. She wasn't one hundred percent back to herself, but she was at a good sixty-five percent, especially since she had gotten a surprise Instagram message from Stefan a few days earlier.

Danielle couldn't believe Stefan was still interested in her. After her failed attempt in 2011, to his attempt in 2013, and now it was 2015 and he sent her a message asking if he could take her out.

She had heard rumors that he was a washed-up old-head who was cheap. Danielle was warned to stay away from him but there was something about him that attracted her, and she couldn't stay away. They had made plans that night for him to come pick her up so they could hang and talk.

"Hey Beautiful, I'm outside," Stefan said on the other end of the phone.

It was raining, but Danielle had a on a black spaghetti strap knee length dress, her furry black closed toe slippers and a black jacket.

Stefan had a few cars, so she didn't know which car to look out for. He flashed his headlights; he was in a tinted black Denali, and she walked over and hopped in the truck.

Once she got in the truck and saw Stefan, her heart started beating fast and her sexual pheromones flared to life. However, she had to act cool.

She was so nervous she didn't know what to say.

"So, what's up?" Stefan said in his low toned voice.

Danielle's heart felt like it was coming out of her chest.

With a smirk on her face she said, "Nothing, much. I'm just glad we were finally able to catch up."

Stefan was looking out his window away from Danielle. She started to feel nervous, the same nervousness she felt at Donny F's party at Feel Good Lounge. *Do I not look cute? Did I say something wrong? Why isn't he giving me all his attention?* She started to question herself.

They stayed quiet for a minute.

"So, what made you want to hit me up?" she asked.

"I just wanted to get to know you I guess."

"Well, I have liked you for so long and just being around you turns me on a lot," Danielle said boldly.

She wanted to get her feelings out the way and tell him what was really on her mind since he was acting a combination of nonchalant and shy.

"I want to fuck you," she blurted out.

"I want to fuck you too," he replied with a grin.

Danielle knew damn well she shouldn't have come on so strong especially on their first meeting, but her hormones were going crazy.

Stefan drove them to his house. Danielle had left Mason with Naja who was now capable of staying home alone with him.

Stefan lived in Tenafly, a ten-minute drive from Danielle's apartment. He had a five-bedroom house. He lived with his mom and had two teenage daughters. Their mother and Stefan had split a few years back, but the girls wanted to stay with him.

Stefan had the basement apartment. It was fully furnished with all updated appliances and fixtures. His bedroom took up half the basement and the other half was his bathroom, where he had a Jacuzzi tub and next to it, he had a standing shower with a rain showerhead and glass doors. His room was painted light grey with a red accent wall where his fifty-five-inch Sony flat screen TV hung. He had gray silk sheets on his king size bed and a black velvet quilt.

"Wow, this is nice," Danielle said, looking around his basement.

"It's something light," Stefan chuckled.

"You can get comfortable, unless what you said in the truck was all talk."

Laughing she replied, "No, what I said is what I meant."

Danielle started to feel the hormones building back up. Her pussy started to cream and her heart started beating faster and faster.

Stefan walked over to her and started kissing her. Danielle wanted to skip the foreplay and jump on him and ride him, but she had to tell herself to calm down.

As he kissed her, he peeled the spaghetti straps off both her shoulders. Her dress fell to the floor. Danielle had no bra or panties on. She had neatly trimmed and shaved her pubic hair down low in the shower just before Stefan arrived outside her place.

His tongue felt so good in her mouth. His spell was like magic. She started to unbutton his shirt while they continued to kiss. His soft black skin felt like leather. Her heart continued to race as her vagina continued to cream without him even touching her.

Stefan pushed her down on the bed where he started kissing on her neck, working his way to her breast, sucking and tracing her areolas with the tip of his tongue.

Danielle started moaning; she knew this was wrong, giving it up so fast, but she had waited for this moment for four years and she didn't give a fuck. All she knew was she wanted Stefan and wasn't going to miss out on losing the opportunity of him being inside of her. He was now kissing her stomach and getting closer and closer to where she wanted him most. He pushed his head down in between her legs. Danielle felt as if she was having a seizure; she couldn't stop shaking. He opened her legs more and delved into her vagina. Stroking his tongue up and down, then sucking on her clitoris. It was the best feeling

Danielle had ever felt and she could've let him go on for hours, but she was ready for the main course. She told him that she wanted to get on top.

Stefan laid on his back. Danielle got on top of him, grabbed his dick and put him inside of her. She started bouncing up and down on top of him. Stefan took his hands and placed them on her breasts and squeezed her areolas which were her weak spots, making her hornier, more wet and her body more attached to his. He was taking a piece of her soul. Danielle had never been so wet, which only served to turn Stefan on even more.

Stefan told her he was about to cum, so Danielle hopped off and put his dick in her mouth and swirled her tongue around it. Then she started sucking his dick, deep throating it more and more. His dick grew bigger and bigger in her mouth. Danielle started make a slurping noise as she inhaled his swollen dick. Stefan grabbed her silky hair and lifted his hips up to sink his dick deeper in her throat and shot a long stream of cum in her mouth. Danielle sucked the remaining cum out of the head of his dick. Stefan collapsed back on the bed. Danielle had never let a man cum in her mouth because she felt that it was nasty but for some reason with Stefan, she loved it. She laid her head on his chest. "I'm sorry I came on so strong, but I wanted you so bad," Danielle said with a low chuckle.

Danielle had literally snatched his soul out from his dick and certainly satisfied his bodily appetite. All he could say in response to her was "Thank you," before placing a kiss on his forehead.

They laid there holding each other, dozing off for a few hours before waking up and Danielle headed back home, feeling like she was floating on cloud nine.

Danielle was in the meeting at work with new perspective sponsors for her company, but she was in a daze. She had a smile on her face all day thinking back to how Stefan made her feel. She barely knew him, but she knew she finally got it right this time when it came to a man. She finally found one that was worthy.

For the first two months of them seeing each other, Danielle kept her relationship with Stefan a secret, but they would text and speak on the phone daily. She would sneak out in the middle of the night to go meet him, and since he had tinted windows, they would sometimes fuck in his truck in her apartment parking lot.

A few months passed and it was now summer. Danielle quit her job as a medical receptionist and started a new job in New York City for a travel magazine as the advertising director. She took a pay cut but got to experience the career she really wanted and got to travel free. Her mom took her kids for the summer so she had more time to spend with Stefan. Things were looking great, for the time being. Danielle finally realized the pay cut she took started to make her late on her rent and she was on the verge of being evicted. Just when she thought she was on her way to the top, strife always seemed to find her.

"Hello."

"Danielle, its Cherry. I wanted to know if I could come over and use your desktop. I'm starting a new business project and I have to type up a few things."

Cherry was Danielle's friend from high school. In high school all the boys liked Cherry because she looked like

Pocahontas with a pretty brown skin tone and long soft silky hair that turned into a bushel of curls when wet. She had a big butt and kept up with the latest fashions. She had taken Danielle under her wing in high school. They had hung out a few times outside of school but were more of just in-school friends.

"Sure, drop by anytime, I'll be home," Danielle replied.

A couple of hours later, Cherry was at Danielle's door. She started working on her project and wanted to catch up with Danielle at the same time, so the girls started talking.

"So, what's going on with you Dee?"

"Just working, the kids left for the summer. I just started a new job, but took a big pay cut and now I'm short on my rent, so I'm just trying to figure out what to do before the kids get back."

Cherry was a social worker in New York City, a bartender at a New York City club on the weekends and modeled for a few clothing brands as well.

"Word. Well if you want, you can come stay at my place until you get your money right and we can go half on the rent. I pay twelve hundred dollars so six hundred dollars apiece."

"Sounds good, but you have a one-bedroom and I don't want to intrude on your space."

"Girl, we will figure it out. You can stay on my sofa and when I go out for the night you can always sleep in my bed."

"Let me think about it and get back to you on that," Danielle replied.

A week later as Danielle was prepping to go on a business trip to Orlando, Florida, she was getting more and more worried about her court date for non-payment of rent that was scheduled for when she returned. The proposition that Cherry offered seemed like her only choice. She thought of asking Stefan for help, but she had never asked a man for help and a man never offered to help her, so she quickly erased that out of her mind. Danielle had lived in shelters, bounced from house to house, and slept on floors in the past and had promised herself she would never allow her son to go through what she put Naja through with moving all around in a non-stable home. She hadn't thought quitting her job for less money all the way through. Times like this were when she wished she had a husband. Someone that would have her back and help direct her to make right decisions, but it was too late for that now and she had to deal with the consequences from the path she chose.

After she returned from her three-day trip to Orlando on Saturday, she prepared herself for court on Monday. When Danielle got to court on Monday, she was able to get all the money needed to pay the past due rent from the local welfare agency but decided to leave the apartment so that she didn't have to worry about being late, or the threat of being evicted.

What the hell, I can go stay with Cherry and save some money and get a bigger and better apartment for me and my kids, Danielle thought to herself.

The following two weeks she started selling her stuff and moving her things into Cherry's apartment.

The kids weren't with Danielle so the move to Cherry's house was great. She was saving money. She and Cherry would go to parties in New York City and get VIP treatment.

Danielle was still talking to Stefan, but things weren't the same because she no longer had her own place and moved an extra twenty minutes away from his house, but they were still in contact daily. She had also ran into Stefan's friend Freeze, who happened to live in the building next to Cherry.

Danielle introduced Freeze to Cherry, and they hit it off almost immediately. Soon Freeze and Cherry were always together, and Danielle was starting to feel like a third wheel. She couldn't understand why Stefan couldn't come through sometimes so they could double date. Freeze had no issue making time for Cherry, despite having a girlfriend of five years according to Alisa, who was friends with Freeze too, due to him being friends with her boyfriend Simon. Alisa showed Danielle Freeze's real girlfriend's Instagram page when Freeze was in the pictures posted three days prior.

Danielle decided to stay out of that drama and chose not to tell Cherry. Cherry had the habit of thinking people were hating on her and wanted to be her, so she didn't want to say anything and have Cherry think she was jealous of the puppy-love her and Freeze had going on.

Work was going well for Danielle; they were sending her to Los Angeles to meet with the Director of Fuji travel and Asiana Airlines to try and get them to buy ad space in the magazine. Danielle still had her raggedy Altima. She drove it to the airport with Cherry and told Cherry she could use it if she really had to, but it was in a desperate need of an oil change. The car was below Cherry's standards so Danielle knew Cherry wouldn't drive it, so she had no worries.

Los Angeles was amazing; Danielle had never been before. Her job booked her a room at the Sofitel, which was a high-class hotel in Beverly Hills. Danielle's meeting with Asiana Airlines didn't go as well as she wanted but she looked forward to the meeting with Fuji's travel director since she had done extensive research on her. She knew she had that meeting in the bag. That night, Cherry called Danielle.

"Danielle, how is your trip going?"

"Girl, I'm having so much fun, but I should be back the day after tomorrow. Is everything ok?"

"Yeah, I'm good, but my mom came over and I had to move your car out of my spot so she could park and when I went to move it back to my spot your car wouldn't start. I called Triple A and they had it towed to the gas station down the street. I think they said the car seized."

"Damn, really? Well, I'm all the way on the west coast, so there's nothing I can do about it from here. I'll check on it soon as I get back," Danielle said with disappointment, as she hung up.

Why the hell would she move the car so her mom could park in her spot briefly? That makes no damn sense. I can't worry about it now, but I can't believe this. Danielle thought to herself.

Danielle went to her meeting. The Fuji director told her she loved her energy and really appreciated her coming in there having read up on her, but she wasn't interested at the present moment in advertising in the magazine since Fuji was more for families and the magazine Danielle worked for focused more on business travel. Danielle was proud that she killed the meeting regardless of not getting the sale. The situation regarding her car kept breaking into her good-spirited thoughts.

As soon as Danielle landed at LaGuardia Airport, she had the Uber driver take her to the gas station where her car was. She tried starting it, but the car wouldn't start. She even had the Uber driver look at her engine to get his opinion, but it wasn't looking good. All the driver could tell her was to return in the morning to speak with the mechanic.

When Danielle got to the apartment, Cherry was in her room.

"Hey, so what happened to my car?"

"Like I told you on the phone, I moved it so that my mom could park in my spot and when I went to move it back it wouldn't start, so I called Triple A for you and had them move it."

"Ok, I'm going to go first thing in the morning and talk to the mechanic."

The next morning, Danielle woke up at 8 AM, having barely slept. "I'm the owner of the black 1997 Nissan Altima. What's wrong with my car?" Danielle asked the guy sitting in the office of the gas station.

"It was brought here for a seized engine."

"Ok, can it be fixed? What do I need to do?"

"Ma'am, your car is done. You can get a new engine, but it will cost you more than what the car is worth."

"I was told my car was only driven from one parking spot to another and it shut off. I can't believe this."

"I've been a mechanic for a long time and that story doesn't even sound legit," the mechanic replied.

"You have to drive a car for at least fifteen to twenty minutes before it starts smoking, then it will seize and shut off. So whoever was driving this car did more than move it from one spot to another; they were driving it."

"So, what can I do?"

"Well, if you leave it here after today, I will start charging you seventy-five dollars a day for storage. The car is junk at this point. Figure out how to get it out of here, otherwise I will start charging you."

Danielle was pissed. Her kids were coming back in a couple of weeks. Her daughter was still going to her old school in Teaneck and they were now in Maywood, which was two towns away. Mason's daycare provider was in Englewood, which was three towns away. Not having a vehicle would make it very difficult to get her kids to school and get to work on time.

As she walked back to Cherry's apartment, she called Alisa to tell her what happened and how the mechanic was implying that Cherry was lying as well as another male acquaintance she spoke to earlier. Once she got inside the apartment, she told Alisa she would call her back.

"The mechanic said that you had to be driving the car for it to shut off. Moving the car from one parking spot to another would not cause the car to seize and you had to be driving it for at least fifteen to twenty minutes," Danielle said to Cherry, wanting a real explanation as to what happened to her car.

Cherry didn't like the fact that she was being accused of lying. She had in fact driven the car to and from a job interview she had for a bartending job at a club in Newark. When she returned home, she parked the car in her assigned spot and when she went to go use it again it didn't start. She wasn't about to pay or give Danielle any money toward that old, raggedy ass car. It was embarrassing enough that she even had to drive the car to her interview.

Cherry raised her eyebrow. "Like I said, I only drove it two minutes. I don't care what the mechanic said, because I know what happened. The car was old and on its last legs anyway, what do you expect?"

Danielle wanted to curse Cherry out, but she was staying in her apartment and had nowhere else to go, so all she could so was walk out to get some air. Danielle got on the phone and called everyone she thought would let her and her kids stay at their place. She started crying more and more on each call, thinking about how she will get her kids around. Then she couldn't help but think of how Cherry didn't even apologize, but said, *"The car was old anyway, what did you expect?"* and was not offering any type of money so that Danielle could take an Uber or a bus to get where she needed to go.

Danielle had called Alisa back and told her what Cherry said and how hurt she was. Alisa couldn't help her out, but she was glad she could be a sympathetic ear for her.

From that day on, the tension between Cherry and Danielle started to fester.

Things started to only get worse for Danielle. The week after she got back from Los Angeles, her job let her go. They weren't making any money and couldn't afford to pay her. So now Danielle was stuck with no car, no job, and no income. At first, she didn't tell Cherry but only told Stefan and Alisa. Danielle would get up every morning and go look for jobs or go over to Alisa's house to sit during the day while she cried and stressed.

It was now the last week of August and the kids were returning the next week. Danielle knew Cherry would be looking for September's rent soon, so she had to tell her she got laid off.

"So, I got laid off yesterday," Danielle said lying.

"What? Why did they lay you off?" Cherry said with an attitude.

"They aren't getting ads sold, so they don't have enough money coming in to pay me."

"Rent is about to be due; I'll see if some of my friends can send me some job openings and I'll forward them to you."

This bitch, Danielle thought. *She had the nerve to lie to me about my car and not apologize or offer me a few bucks yet get an attitude with me when I told her I got laid off? I am not paying her shit, fuck that!*

The following week Danielle's mom returned the kids. Danielle started taking Mason back to the sitter, crying as she walked the five blocks to the bus stop every morning. She left Naja behind since school hadn't started yet so that gave her at least a week to figure out how she was going to drop off both the kids in the morning.

After dropping Mason off in the morning, she would head over to her cousin's house who lived near the sitter and vent to them how she was pissed and needed a car. It just so happened, her cousin's girlfriend was selling her 2000 Nissan Altima and since they were family, he would sell it to her for seven hundred dollars.

Danielle had one more check coming in from the magazine. It was for eighteen hundred dollars, so she told her cousin give her a few days and she would return with the money. Danielle knew for a fact she wasn't going to give Cherry a dime.

"Mom," Naja whispered to Danielle as Cherry was in her room.

"What?"

"How much longer do we have to stay here? I don't like Cherry. She wants me to clean the mess she leaves behind in the kitchen when you aren't here, and she was drinking Mason's juice."

"I told her not to drink his juice," Danielle sighed. "We will be out of here soon; I'm working on it."

It was bad enough that Danielle had heard that Cherry told Freeze that Naja was lazy and had no respect, but now Naja was telling her that Cherry wanted her to clean up after her and was drinking her baby's juice. Danielle had to call Alisa and vent. Danielle wasn't saying anything that wasn't true about Cherry; the girl kept her house a mess, dishes piled up in the sink, marijuana roaches all over the living room where Danielle was sleeping with her kids and the car incident, and when she cooked, she only cooked for herself or for Freeze, despite the fact Danielle was letting her use her food stamp card. Danielle was over it. She started to deeply regret the decision she made to leave her apartment and move in with Cherry. Things would have worked themselves out if she had allowed them to instead of jumping the gun and moving in with Cherry.

Alisa was always a sympathetic ear and so was Stefan. The situation with Cherry made Danielle long for Stefan more because he was the only thing that made her feel good, and when they spoke, he was always uplifting her.

A couple of days later Cherry told Danielle to come outside on the balcony that she needed to speak to her.

"Is everything okay, between me and you?"

"Yeah, why?" Danielle asked.

"I just wanted to make sure you were okay. If you have any issues with me or whatever, you can tell me and let me know."

Danielle found it weird that Cherry was asking her those questions, like she knew Danielle was unhappy living with her.

Danielle knew Freeze and Stefan were best friends, but her and Stefan liked each other and were intimate for the past six months. *He couldn't be going and telling Freeze everything they talked about privately? Or was he?* Danielle was starting to feel betrayed by Stefan. Danielle texted Alisa.

Hey Alisa, I need to talk.

Hey, D, you okay?

Yeah, I just need to come over tomorrow after you get off work for some wine and girl talk.

Sure, come over any time after four, I'll be here.

Ok, boo, see you tomorrow. Thank you and goodnight.

The next day Danielle took a cab over to Alisa's house. Alisa lived on a dead-end street in Teaneck. On her way over to Alisa's house she passed the street she once lived on with her mom and her mom's first husband. Life was so fun back then; as a family they spent a lot of time doing things together. She wished she could've given her children that same experience instead of moving all over the place and dealing with all sorts of drama. If only she could turn back the hands of time.

"What's up girl? You sounded stressed on the phone."

Taking a deep breath, Danielle said, "I want to get out of Cherry's apartment right now. This bitch fucked up my car, never apologized, never offered me any money, is drinking my baby's juice, doesn't clean up after herself and last night she asked if I had anything to tell her, like she knows I'm talking about her or something. If I wasn't staying in her place, I would tell her how I feel, but since I have nowhere else to go, I don't want to make the situation worse than it is."

"That's fucked up she did you like that, D. What are you planning on doing?"

"I don't know yet, but I called Stefan over so I can talk to him outside because I think he is telling Freeze stuff, and Freeze must be going back and telling Cherry."

The two sipped on their wine and Alisa was catching Danielle up on the local gossip and what was going on between her and Simon.

I'm outside. Read the text from Stefan as she sat in Alisa's kitchen.

"Stefan is outside. Let me go talk to him really quick."

Danielle headed for the door.

"Mom, where are you going?" asked Naja, who was sitting in Alisa's living room with Mason watching TV.

"I got to go outside to talk to a friend, I'll be right back."

Danielle hopped in Stefan's truck with a smile on her face. The immediate presence of Stefan always made her blush.

They gave each other a kiss on the lips.

"What did you have to talk to me about?" Stefan asked.

"Well, I wanted to know why you are telling Freeze everything I am telling you about Cherry. She came up to me last night asked if there was anything on my mind that I needed to tell her, like she knows I've been talking about her."

"You know Freeze is my best friend, but whatever we discuss I don't repeat to anybody. You need to ask your friend Alisa that question, not me."

"What do you mean, ask Alisa?"

"You know Alisa and Freeze talk on the phone almost every day, and if I'm not telling Freeze it might just be her."

Danielle started to think back on the last few weeks. Alisa was always asking about what was going on with her and Cherry. Danielle thought she was asking because she was a concerned friend. At the same time, Danielle started questioning Alisa's friendship. Alisa had a spare room and never offered

Danielle the space. Alisa did gossip about other people to Danielle, but Danielle would have never guessed her good friend of six years would go and repeat anything she told her about Cherry. What was her motive? She didn't even know Cherry.

"What? I didn't know they spoke on the phone every day."

"Yeah, they are always talking," answered Stefan.

"Why, would Freeze go back and tell Cherry though? We are cool and he has a girlfriend and I haven't gone back and told Cherry that," Danielle questioned.

"I don't know love, but just be careful who you vent to, and just know it wasn't me. I would never to that to you."

"Let me get back inside. I'll call you later," Danielle said, before kissing Stefan goodbye.

"You and Stefan good?" Alisa asked, as she walked back into the kitchen.

"We are good. He told me he wasn't telling anyone anything we discuss, and that Cherry was probably just reading my energy," Danielle replied, not trusting Alisa's question.

Danielle had decided to sleep over at Alisa's house. Remembering what Stefan had said, Danielle made sure to be careful what she said to Alisa from then on.

Danielle went to pick up the car her cousin Andre sold her. "Cuz, you still need a place to stay?" Andre asked.

Andre wanted to help his cousin out as much as he could.

"Yeah, I'm trying to get out of this girl's place ASAP." "Jenny and I got a two-bedroom. You and your kids can stay with us until you get back on your feet."

That was all Danielle needed to hear; she agreed.

Danielle had registered the car the day before. She hopped in it and drove back to Cherry's apartment. She decided not to tell Cherry she got a new car.

The next week while Cherry was at work, Danielle started to take her things out of the apartment. After she removed everything, she left Cherry a note thanking her and left the key under the welcome mat.

Andre lived in Lodi, New Jersey. It was farther out but Danielle had a car now, so she didn't mind the extra travel to drop off the kids.

Andre and his wife didn't charge her to stay with them, but she still need to make money.

Danielle answered an ad on Craigslist looking for dancers in Northern New Jersey. She called Rob, who was the contact name on the job posting. Rob told her to text him some photos of how she looked. Once she did, he texted her back and told her she could start that night. He told her to go to Gentlemen's Lounge at 435 Main Street in East Orange.

Danielle had never stripped or even thought about stripping, but she needed the money and needed it fast. With the last forty dollars she had, she bought a G-string bathing suit and some heels. Thankfully, after school, Naja would pick up Mason up from the sitter and they would go to Danielle's aunt's house, so Danielle picked up the kids and then dropped them off at Andre's house.

"I got to go make some money, so keep an eye on Mason," Danielle said, after she let the kids into the apartment.

Danielle gassed up her car with the remaining ten dollars she had and headed to her new job.

Danielle was nervous as she headed into the gentlemen's club. She signed in with the club manager, Sly. Sly was a heavyset Portuguese man. He looked like he belonged on an episode of the Sopranos, Danielle thought. He asked what her stage name was. Danielle didn't know she needed a stage name, but the name Coco came to her off the top of her head.

"Ok, Coco, you will go out with Diamond and Star, fifteen after every hour. You will dance on stage for fifteen minutes, then when you're done you can collect the money that was thrown at you, then go around the bar and entertain the guest for tips. If a guest wants the VIP room, you take him back and do whatever your limit is, but no sex. For the first song you charge them twenty dollars, and if you're still in VIP after the first song, you can charge them whatever you want. Real simple," Sly said.

Danielle headed to the changing room, where she encountered five other girls.

"You must be new, I never seen you around here before." Danielle heard from a voice in the corner.

Danielle turned around and saw a short Spanish girl about five-one with long black hair, a big butt and big breasts getting dressed.

"I'm Star."

Star had a pretty face with hazel eyes and a tattoo all over her back.

"I'm Coco, and yes, today is my first day ever stripping," Danielle said, with a nervous chuckle.

"If you know how to fuck, then you should be fine on stage. Act like that pole is your man, that's the best advice for a newbie," Star said, as she laughed.

"I'm going on stage when you do, so I'll follow your lead."

"Okay, but I suggest you take a few shots of your favorite drink to boost your confidence," Star said, as she headed toward the door to start her shift.

Danielle went over to the bar and ordered three shots of Patron before heading onstage. She never danced on a pole; she didn't know how to do the tricks she had seen other females do. Her outfit was cheesy compared to what everyone else had on. After she finished her shots, she walked on stage for her first fifteen minutes. Some upbeat song was on that she wasn't familiar with, but she placed one hand on the pole and did some twirls and then shook her ass for the crowd. She repeated that over and over, adding a few different moves that involved bending up and down and twerking. That was the longest fifteen minutes she ever experienced in her life and that was the first, she had to do it six more times.

After she finished each time, she came off stage and went around to flirt with the guests, pulling down her top quickly so they could see her breasts and want to tip. On her third week, an older African man named Tommy took her to the VIP room.

Danielle saw some of the other girls back there getting their titties sucked or getting what looked like them getting fingered as she walked past each booth peeking through the curtain. Danielle didn't want any man touching her like that. She hadn't told Stefan she was stripping but she wasn't willing to jeopardize her self-respect more then she felt she already had by having men touch her in her sexual spots.

Danielle sat Tommy down and started grinding on him. Tommy kept complimenting how beautiful she was and how he would love to take her home. Danielle just let him talk as she continued to grind on him, then Tommy tried to finger her. She ended the session and took the one hundred dollars he owed her, grabbed her clothes out the dressing room and left the club crying. She hated the fact that she was dancing and being seductive, had to pay a house fee, and men thinking they could just touch her any way they wanted. She needed the money, but this couldn't be the only way. She sat in her car and cried.

Why can't I find a man that loves me? A man that will make sure I'm good and we can live together. He will have my back and I will have his. I just want someone that truly cares about me. Why is it so hard for me to find what I want and need? All Danielle wanted was to have a man that loved her and wanted to marry her so that she could be that happy, submissive wife that she felt every good man deserved. She wanted that from Stefan. He constantly gave her mixed signals. *Does he like me, or just want to fuck me? Why can't he be the man I know I deserve?* Danielle sat in the car for another five minutes before Sly came knocking on the window.

"What's going on? Why did you leave? You have to go get back on stage and don't forget you have to pay the house fee before you leave!"

"I don't feel good, my stomach hurts. I can't continue tonight, and I didn't make enough to pay the house fee for tonight."

"Okay, well you can leave. I will let you slide tonight but next time I need the money."

Chapter 12

The next day, Danielle called her mom crying and told her she was ready to change her life and wanted to come home. All Danielle's mom wanted was for her daughter to find God for herself, pray and become spiritually motivated in life. Danielle's mom Maria and her husband Colin agreed to have Danielle and the kids come live with them in North Carolina if Danielle went to church and kept the house clean, which Danielle and Naja both agreed to do.

Living in a religious home, Danielle knew that fornication would not be allowed. The only person Danielle was sexing was Stefan, so she had no issue giving up sex. As long as she was communicating with Stefan, she was happy.

Living with her mom was a relief; everyone had their own room in her mom's four-bedroom, three level townhouse. Her mom had a washer and dryer, there was a pool in the community, a basketball court, a gym and a great living environment.

Danielle got to learn how to cook different recipes, she lost all her remaining fat from being pregnant with Mason, and she was going to church and reading her bible. Her relationship with her mother was improving and everything was going great. The only thing Danielle wanted now was a family of her own; she had the kids but was still missing the husband.

Good morning, Beautiful, texted Stefan.

He would text her weekly and it made her feel good, but when she texted or called him back, she wouldn't get an answer or response, but would see Stefan on Instagram posting pictures or commenting on a mutual friend's post. When she did talk to Stefan and told him how she felt, he would say he was at work posting, which only took a second, or he was busy with his kids or sleeping.

The same second Stefan took to post an Instagram post or reply to someone else's post he could have responded to her text; she knew he was free more than he claimed. Danielle knew Stefan must have found himself another friend to satisfy his desires since Danielle was no longer around.

Stefan liked Danielle but he was unsure of what the future held for them. He was a grown man, who a lot of women threw themselves at. He could have anyone he wanted. Danielle was cute but she could be clingy at times and she wasn't where he would have liked her to be in life and she didn't allow him to chase her, which was a turn-off because he loved a challenge.

Danielle wanted to return to New Jersey because she felt as if she was missing out on her chance with Stefan being so far away and being friends with him on social media was making her emotional since he continued to give it more attention than he did her. She thought if she moved back, he would give her the attention she wanted from him.

Donny F was throwing an all-white party, Day Party, at Club Bliss the last week in May 2016 and Danielle made plans to go to New Jersey so she could go. She knew Stefan would be there along with Freeze.

Danielle made plans with Toya to meet up for the party once she got into town the morning of the party.

Danielle headed to Paterson to get a quick weave done, then headed to Toya's house to get dressed. Danielle wore some white jeans with a white tank and blue high heels.

Soon as she and Toya got to Bliss, Danielle was looking out for Freeze's black truck with black tinted windows or Stefan's blue Ferrari he had brought while Danielle was in North Carolina.

As they parked the car and headed toward the entrance of the club, Danielle spotted Freeze's distinct black Escalade and she started to get anxious because she was about to see Stefan; his presence always gave her butterflies.

It was crowded when they walked in. They headed for the bathroom to make sure they were looking right, then headed to the bar. From the bar, you could see who was coming in and everyone in VIP by the DJ booth. There, she spotted the finest, darkest chocolate brother in the club, Stefan. At first Danielle just watched him. She wanted to know if he was with a female or giving anyone attention. Once she saw he was just casually talking to different people, she was about to walk up to him when she saw him stop and talk to a female. Danielle wasn't sure of what was being said, but soon as Stefan walked away from the female, she saw him head to the bar and get two drinks.

"Oh, hey babe, what's up? Who is that drink for?"

"Hey, Beautiful," Stefan replied suavely. "It's for you."

Danielle knew that was a lie because she didn't drink dark liquor, especially not Remy. However, she took the drink, hoping the female he really ordered the drink for saw her down it.

Stefan hung with Danielle at the party, taking shots of Remy, which got Danielle super horny.

"Did you drive your car, or did you ride with Freeze?" Danielle asked.

"I drove my Ferrari. It's out front."

"I want to go to your car for a minute," Danielle replied.

Stefan knew exactly what Danielle wanted to do in his car. Stefan knew Danielle wanted to give him some head and he wouldn't pass that up because Danielle always made him cum when she sucked him off.

They went out to the car

"Daddy, you know I miss you."

"Well, show Daddy how much you missed him then," Stefan said with a smirk.

He gave Danielle a lingering kiss and took her hand and placed it on his dick.

Danielle unzipped his pants as they continued to kiss. Once unzipped, she pulled out his shaft. She then wrapped her lips around the tip of his dick and started sucking it as she slid both her hands up and down his dick. Her saliva made it easy for her hands to glide up and down his shaft and when she felt it was slippery enough, she started to deep throat his dick bobbing her mouth up and down. Stefan had his eyes closed moaning while Danielle used her hands to massage his balls at the same time.

Knowing she was satisfying him, made Danielle wet.

Whenever she gave Stefan head, he made it seem like he was in control, but it was really Danielle in control and that's what she liked. It only took Danielle six minutes to make Stefan nut.

After getting themselves together, they headed back into the party until last call.

Danielle knew her and Stefan would get it together. She was planning on moving back and she just gave him the best head.

A week later Danielle took all the money she had and rented a two-bedroom apartment in Teaneck. She had been talking to Stefan for a little over a year and now that she was back things would get serious, and hopefully marriage would soon come into play. Despite the fact that Stefan was a cheapskate, Danielle loved him for him.

After Danielle was settled, Stefan would come by and see her just because he missed her. However that lasted for only a week, then Stefan returned to the short text messages or not answering messages she sent, but continually made time for Instagram.

"Stefan, can we go out for drinks? I just want to see you and send time with you," Danielle said on the phone.

"We can do that. Where you want to go?"

"Regina's Steakhouse on Teaneck Road tonight at 7 PM. I'll call you when I'm heading out."

"Ok, Beautiful, see you later."

Danielle put her quick weave into a bun and her bangs covering her forehead. She wore an all-black maxi dress and some summer sandals.

RING, RING, RING, RING "You have reached 555-755-9763. The person you are calling cannot come to the phone right now, please leave a message after the tone."

Danielle called Stefan three more times, getting his voicemail all three times.

She then texted him, *Hello, are you still meeting me, because I'm on my way to Regina's.*

Stefan texted, *My daughters just came back from vacation with their mother, so I'm not coming out right now.*

Danielle knew he wanted to spend time with his daughters—he was such a great father—however, he was going out any other time, but every time it was with her there was always an excuse. He had agreed earlier, but now he couldn't. All Danielle could do was cry. She had told Naja she was going out with Stefan, but she didn't want her daughter to know she got stood up, so she headed out to Regina's by herself crying on her way.

Summer was now winding down. Danielle had settled back in New Jersey but her plans of her and Stefan living happily ever after wasn't going as planned. She was getting down on herself again because she couldn't get her life, especially her love life, together. Donny F was throwing a 2016 End of the Summer Party at Bliss Lounge again. Danielle was excited to go since she had been moping around. Danielle called Lisa, who she hadn't hung out with in so long, to see if she wanted to go with her,

"Girl, everybody from Bergen County, Passaic County and Harlem is going to be there."

"Word, I'm definitely done. I need to find me a new boo anyway and those Harlem niggas are some kind of different," Lisa chuckled.

Danielle knew Stefan and Freeze were going to be there in the VIP section popping bottles like they always did when they went to a party.

The party was three days away. Danielle had to make sure she looked cute so that dudes would holler, and Stefan would see she had options.

Danielle got a neck length quick weave done, an acrylic French manicure, a pedicure, some killer navy-blue high heels from Nine West and a few jewelry accessories from Forever 21 that matched her shoes perfectly.

Lisa picked up Danielle in her Red Acura RLX the day of the party. Danielle was excited and anxious. The excitement of seeing Stefan was on her mind.

"Hey girl, you look cute. You definitely going to leave tonight with some numbers," Lisa said, with a laugh when Danielle entered the car.

"Girl, bye. I will only be having my eye on one guy and you know who that is."

"You still feeling Stefan?" Lisa said, as she shook her head. "You can do so much better. Yeah he is handsome, a good father and has his shit together, but after that he is shallow. You said he has yet to take you out or spend any real quality time with you, but yet he has time to pop bottles in the VIP section of every big, local party with Freeze like they are twenty when those niggas are forty-something years old."

"I know, I know, but there is something about him that I like."

"Well, let's go. Hopefully he will have you in VIP with him or at least buy you a drink," Lisa laughed, as she pulled off.

The line outside of Bliss was extensive as the two pulled up. Danielle noticed Freeze's new Mercedes Benz G Class truck parked near the club entrance and knew Stefan must already be there as well.

Lisa found a spot in the rear of the building. The two got out, fixed their outfits, made sure each looked up to par and took a few selfies before heading to the door. Once they walked up to the entrance, the line had died down. Donny F was at the door greeting people as they entered. He gave both the girls a hug once they reached him before entering. Donny F was always friendly and always showed love to those who showed love to him.

The girls finally entered the club. DJ T Moody from Paterson was playing his set. Danielle and Lisa headed to the bathroom to look in the full-length mirror before heading back out to the bar. Once at the bar, Danielle started looking around. Next to the DJ booth was the VIP section and Danielle spotted Stefan and Freeze.

In the meantime, Lisa was socializing, getting her and Danielle free drinks from random dudes she was sitting next to at the bar.

"Girl, would you stop worrying about that man and take these free drinks I'm getting for us."

"I'm not worried about him; I'm just checking out the crowd."

Laughing, Lisa said, "OK bitch, whatever. Let's down these drinks and get on the dance floor because that DJ is rocking."

Once on the dance floor, Danielle spotted Stefan again. She wasn't sure if he saw her yet because he had yet to say anything to her. She noticed him surrounded by a group of females and he was laughing too hard in her eyes to whatever they were discussing. Danielle distracted herself by engaging in conversation with one of the guys that bought her a drink.

"Damn Ma, you have a real exotic look to you. Where are

you from?" The guy was about five-ten, 190 pounds, light skinned and had beautiful wavy hair just how Danielle really liked her men.

"To tell you the truth, I hate that question. I get it a lot and at the end of the day I'm Black mixed with a bunch of stuff."

"My bad, Ma. I was just trying to make conversation."

"It's all good, but thank you for the drink. Imma head over to the other bar and join my cousin." Danielle was over him and his lame-ass attempt at conversation.

As she headed over to Lisa, Stefan spotted her.

He knew if he didn't speak, he would have to hear her whining another day and he wasn't beat for her emotional antics.

As Danielle was sipping on her coconut Cîroc with pineapple juice, Stefan walked up beside her. She couldn't believe that he walked up on her.

The two stood by the bar together talking, when T Moody put on "Sex with Me" by Rhianna. Danielle started grinding on Stefan.

As the two were dancing, a woman walked over and started questioning Stefan about who Danielle was. Danielle had never seen her before; she was light skinned, older than Danielle, not that attractive and was highly intoxicated.

Stefan looked at the female like she was stupid.

"Is there a problem?" Danielle asked the female.

"Yes, but it has nothing to do with you."

"If I'm dancing with my boo and you come over here getting in his face, it does have to do with me!"

"Let's go, Natalie," her friends said. She acted as if she didn't want to go but they pulled her away and out of the club.

"Who the fuck was that?" Danielle questioned Stefan.

"That was nobody, some chick I use to mess with. It ain't nothing to worry about."

"What are you doing later? I want to see you," Danielle asked.

"Freeze and I are going uptown, but I'll hit you up and we will link."

Stefan gave her a kiss, then Danielle went to find Lisa who was standing near the exit talking to some dudes.

"Are you done boo-loving over there, damn?"

"Yes," Danielle said laughing.

"Well, this is Tone and Earl; they want to hit up another party. You want to go?"

"Sure, I'm down."

They four of them headed to Regina's Steakhouse. The whole time, Danielle kept checking her phone to see if Stefan had called or texted. The guys kept buying drinks for the girls. Lisa had stopped drinking because she still had to drop Danielle off and then drive home, so Danielle was drinking both her and Lisa's drinks. Her mind kept fantasizing about Stefan.

It was going on 1:30 AM and Regina's was about to close. Danielle still hadn't heard from Stefan.

She decided to text him, *Hey, what's up?*

It was now 2 AM and Stefan still hadn't replied to her text. Lisa had dropped Danielle off. Danielle was fixated on seeing Stefan, so she got in her car and drove past Stefan's house. His Ferrari wasn't there, so she knew he was still out. So she parked her car near the front of his house and texted him again.

Am I going to see you?

Danielle waited ten minutes and no response. She then called him; after four rings his voicemail came on.

Danielle sat in her car and started crying. *What am I doing wrong?* she thought to herself. *I thought he liked me. I thought he was different.* Danielle continued to cry for about another ten minutes before she pulled off and headed home.

Chapter 13

The next day, Englewood was having their Annual Whip Whop Basketball game in Morris Park, where locals play in a tournament in memory of a local Englewood resident that passed away; they also have food and give away school supplies. Danielle had volunteered to help set up for the event. Everyone that was at the Day Party the day before, was also at the game. While supplying the players with water, Danielle noticed three cars pull in the parking lot and drive right up on the grass where cars weren't permitted. It was a Mercedes Benz G class, a blue Ferrari and an all-black Mercedes SL 400. Danielle knew immediately that it was Freeze, Stefan and Simon. Her heart started throbbing in her chest again.

She continued handing out water to the players, when she heard a voice.

"Hey, Beautiful."

Danielle was mad he stood her up and ignored her call and

texts. But she couldn't help but blush when she heard his voice. She turned her head and said what's up to Freeze, then turned and looked at Stefan and with a smirk she replied, "Fuck You."

Stefan laughed, and replied, "You're still beautiful."

Danielle walked off. *Why does he play with me like that?* she thought to herself.

Danielle spent the rest of the game hanging with her cousins but kept an eye on Stefan up until the game was over.

Three weeks had passed since the basketball game and that was the last time she spoke or saw Stefan. It had been three months since they were sexually involved. She was starting to feel it was time to move on from Stefan since he didn't make her a priority. She had since started a job at the local hospital doing overnight security and a day job working as a waitress at a new brick oven pizzeria in Englewood.

Danielle had a few weeks left alone before her mom would drop Naja and Mason off since the summer was coming to an end and school would be starting soon.

One night she didn't go work and wanted to hang out, she remembered Mike had hit her up on IG direct message while she was in North Carolina and told to her to hit him up when she got back in town. She logged into her Instagram account and decided to hit him up.

Hey Mike, I'm back in town. We can hang out if you're free.

Mike sent his number and told her to call.

Danielle called; after two rings it went to voicemail.

She DM'd Mike back

I just called you, no answer.

Thirty seconds later she got a phone call from Mike.

"Hey Lady, what's up?"

"Nothing much. I was calling to take you up on our offer of getting a few drinks."

"Meet me at G&G's. I should be there in ten minutes," Mike replied.

G&G's was a liquor store in Teaneck about three minutes away from Danielle's house. It had a small bar in the back that Danielle never hung out at.

Danielle pulled up to the back of the liquor store where the entrance to the bar was. She waited inside her 2000 four-door black Honda Civic until Mike hit her up.

"I'm here, where are you?"

"You're actually walking past my car now," Danielle giggled.

She exited her car and greeted Mike and the two headed inside and ordered a few drinks. Everyone knew Mike, so everyone that walked in came over to where the two were and showed him love.

Despite the fact that Danielle didn't care for how he pulled out knots of money and his teeth were a little jacked, he was cute and charismatic and funny.

The two stepped outside to smoke their Newport shorts. As they were smoking, Danielle asked Mike where he was in his IG post with the Jacuzzi.

"The Skyview Motel in Fort Lee. Nobody knows about that spot, it's in the cut."

"I want to sit up in the Jacuzzi and relax. I always wondered where you go."

"We can go now if you want," Mike replied.

"Oh, for real? Yeah, we can do that."

They hopped in Danielle's car and headed to the Skyview Motel in Fort Lee. Danielle never seen or heard of the motel. It was located on Bergen Boulevard, five minutes from the George Washington Bridge heading into New York City.

Mike got the key to the room and drove around the building to park. When Danielle stepped in the room, she was amazed. It was a motel, which she always thought were dingy, but it had marble floors, an updated bathroom and a nice big Jacuzzi with a brick wall on two sides and a big glass mirror positioned directly behind the Jacuzzi.

Mike set up the water and bubble bath for Danielle, while she got comfortable.

Danielle went into the bathroom, took off her clothes and wrapped a towel around her. She exited the bathroom and sat on the bed until the water was ready. Mike left the room to go get ice and Danielle hopped into the Jacuzzi. She didn't want Mike to see her naked because she didn't want him to get the wrong idea.

When Mike came back into the room, Danielle was laying covered in bubbles, relaxing.

Mike sat in the lounge area, watching TV and rolling a blunt on the table. The two chatted on and off in the meantime.

After thirty minutes, Danielle got out, grabbed the towel she had lying next to the Jacuzzi and wrapped it around her.

She walked over to the bed and asked Mike for a Newport. They both smoked a cigarette.

"Can you do me a favor, Mike?

"Depends on what it is," Mike laughed.

"I sleep naked, so I don't want you to get any ideas, but can you give me a massage?"

160

Laughing, Mike replied, "Yeah, that's not a problem."

Mike shut off the light but kept the TV on. He walked over to the bed where Danielle was laying. She was on her stomach so her back and bare ass was facing him. He took some of the motel lotion, rubbed it on his hands and started massaging Danielle's back. He worked his way down to her ass. She felt so relaxed and enjoyed the feeling.

After ten minutes of him massaging her up and down while she on her stomach, he told her to flip over to that he could massage her breasts and stomach.

Mike cupped her breasts with his hands massaging them, then he worked his way down to her pussy.

"Move up a little," Mike whispered.

Danielle moved up closer to the top of the bed as Mike massaged her thighs.

Suddenly Danielle felt Mike's tongue in between her legs.

"Ohhh, what are you doing?" Danielle asked, while being surprised.

Mike didn't answer, rather his tongue plunged deeper in Danielle pussy. She started moaning. She grabbed Mike by his head; she wanted him to devour her pussy. Danielle hadn't gotten her pussy ate in so long and Mike made it feel so good.

"Oh my god," Danielle moaned repeatedly.

Mike got on top of Danielle and started kissing her. Danielle sucked on his tongue while he slid his dick into her wet-ass pussy.

Mike took her leg and lifted it up to get his dick inside of her better.

Danielle could feel Mike had a big dick. Danielle grabbed his shaft with her pussy and squeezed it around his dick; Mike started to moan. He started thrusting his dick inside of her harder and harder. Danielle was about to cum; she told him to slow down. She grabbed his butt and gyrated her hips continuously holding his dick with her pussy in slow motion. Mike started kissing her neck and tonguing her until she finally started to scream, because she was coming. Mike's dick was so wet when he pulled it out of her. He wiped his dick off with the towel Danielle had on the bed. Danielle got up and went to the bathroom to wipe herself off. She returned to the bed and laid next to Mike who wrapped his arm around her until the two dozed off to sleep.

Aunt Lorraine was watching the kids for her most of the time, so that left her and Mike a lot of time to spend together. Danielle barely went home ,and when she did it was to take a shower, get a change of clothes and drop off clean clothes for the kids. Danielle was starting to like Mike, but she wished it was Stefan she was with. Mike called her every day. He brought food to her at work when she was hungry. They went out to restaurants to eat daily; she would hang out with him and his friends and he made her laugh. Danielle felt like she finally found the one. Despite the fact Mike sold drugs for a living and didn't have a home of his own, he was someone she was willing to give a chance.

"What is it that we are doing?" Danielle asked Mike one morning after they'd just had sex.

"I don't know, it's only been a month. It's whatever the universe decides. One day at a time."

Danielle was willing to go slow, but she couldn't wait for Naja and Mason to meet Mike. One day the four of them took a trip to the mall. Danielle was excited to hear what Naja had to say about Mike. Naja wasn't a fan of Stefan because he always seemed to make her mom cry or upset. After the day at the mall, Naja though Mike was nice and funny, and her mom seemed happy and that was what she like to see.

Danielle soon started a new job in New York City thanks to her high school friend, Ebony. Danielle was working for a well-known hospitality company and handled new business accounts; some days she would work twelve hours. In between work and making sure she was spending time with her kids, her time with Mike was getting shorter. They had been kicking it for forty days, but it was the best forty days she ever had.

Danielle had her day off during the week. So she and Mike decided to go to a motel in Little Ferry to spend some time away together.

Danielle picked Mike up, checked into the room and smoked a blunt in the bathroom. Danielle started to sense some distance from Mike. Something didn't seem right. After smoking, she laid in the bed and went on Instagram, while Mike laid on the sofa and was on his phone laughing. Danielle wanted to have Mike's attention.

"Babe, I'm horny," she said.

"Really, Danielle? You always want sex," Mike chuckled.

"C'mon please, before I go to bed, I got to get up early for work."

Mike put his phone down and walked over to the bed. He got on top of her before putting her in the doggy style position, which made him cum in five min. He waited for Danielle to orgasm before he slapped her ass and said, "You happy now?"

Danielle dozed off to sleep with Mike back on his phone.

The alarm went off at 6:30 AM. Mike was still asleep.

163

Danielle got up and dressed. She woke Mike to tell him she was leaving and gave him a kiss goodbye.

Two days had passed. Mike had texted Danielle, but she wasn't getting her morning phone calls, or her "*Are you hungry*" texts. Danielle was starting to feel confused.

On her next day off she went to G&G's bar to see if she would run into him. After sitting there for an hour and throwing back drink after drink, Mike finally walked in.

"Hey Lady," Mike said, when he saw her in the corner seat by the door.

"Hey, Mike. We need to talk."

"I just came here to meet somebody, but I got to make a run. I'll be back in a few, we can talk then?"

"Okay," Danielle replied.

Danielle waited and waited and was getting more drunk by the minute. The bar was about to close and still no sign of Mike. She called him, but he didn't answer.

When she got home, she called him again and again. No answer. Danielle really couldn't understand what happened between them.

Danielle was starting to feel "off" within herself. She was hitting him up constantly on social media, just to see that he had "*seen*" her messages and not replied. She kept texting and calling his phone, and nothing. She wanted him to tell her what happened. What did she do wrong?

Danielle started to think that maybe she wasn't off, but maybe she was pregnant. Danielle brought a pregnancy test even though she knew it would be too early for a positive result. The test came out negative. She was relieved but she wanted to know what the hell was going on within herself.

Four more days passed, and Danielle brought another pregnancy test since her period was four days away, she knew the early pregnancy test would detect if she was or not.

She peed on the stick and waited for the results. After a minute, a faint line appeared. Danielle couldn't believe it. She was pregnant again, which helped explain her crazy stalkish behavior, but she wasn't in the right place to have another baby. Mason was only three years old and she didn't want another baby right now. Danielle figured she would tell Mike and he would understand her behavior and they could work out whatever issue he had with her and they could do things the right way and have the family life she craved with someone she loved.

Danielle knew Mike wasn't answering her calls, so she sent him a message on Instagram:

Hey Mike, I know you aren't talking to me and I still don't know why, but I just took a pregnancy test, and it came out positive. Call me when you can so we can discuss this.

Danielle kept checking her the message to see if Mike had seen the message. Three minutes after she sent him the message, he seen it. However, still no reply.

Another week had passed and still no word from Mike. She didn't want to let anyone in on her secret. One day, bored at work, she posted a picture on Instagram of her feet kicked up on her work desk. About an hour after posting, she saw that Mike had liked the picture.

How the hell can he like my stupid picture but can't reply to my messages that I'm pregnant with his baby. She said to herself.

Danielle got more pissed but had to cover up her emotions while at work.

When she got home that evening, she needed to vent, so she called Toya.

"Hey cuz, what's up?" Toya answered.

"I just got home from my new job in the city, but I've been stressing!"

"Stressing, what's up?"

"Well Mike has been acting weird. He hasn't called or texted me ever since I broke the news to him that I am pregnant."

"Wait, what? Pregnant?"

"Yes, cuz. I didn't want to tell anyone yet, but I don't know where to turn, especially since he liked a post I put on IG but doesn't have the nerve to reply to my messages."

"What the hell is wrong with him?" Toya questioned.

"I don't know, but it's really starting to piss me off more."

"Maybe you need to go by his house?" Toya suggested.

"Maybe I should. I don't understand why a grown man is acting like a sixteen-year-old boy. He never showed that side of him to me, but again, like in his words I only knew him for forty days," Danielle said, as she shook her head.

"You know how these men are, always trying to manipulate a female. Girl, you're better than me. Give him a little more time to respond to you, but if not, definitely considering going to his house. I got to get back to work, but I'll talk to you later."

The two hung up.

Danielle thought about it. Two days later she went to Mike's house. She sat in the car for a minute, wondering if she should really go knock on his momma's door. She was thirty-five years old and she had to go knock on the door of a thirty-nine-year-old man because he wouldn't answer her calls or text. She felt like a little high school girl having to do this bullshit. However, she wanted to talk to him and if this was the only way to reach him, she would have to do it.

Danielle got out the car and walked to the front door. She rang the doorbell and a few seconds passed before she saw his mother opening the door.

"Hello, I can I help you?" she asked.

"Hi, I'm looking for Mike. Is he here?"

"No, he isn't."

"Well, can you relay a message to him? I have been trying to call and text him, but he isn't answering. I am pregnant and I need to speak to him," Danielle blurted out.

His mother sighed, "Y'all are two grown adults. You could've kept your legs closed and I don't want this drama at my door. I ain't taking care of no more kids."

I don't know what type of girls he's dealt with in the past, but I'm definitely not trying to bring drama to her or nobody else. Those days are over for me. I don't need nobody to take care of my kids, Danielle thought to herself.

"I understand Ma'am, I just want him to call me."

"Okay, like I said, I will tell him. What he does after that I have nothing to do with."

"Okay, thank you," Danielle said, and his mother closed the door. Danielle headed back to her car and took a deep breath.

Mike never called Danielle.

Weeks went by. Danielle called him a few times and got through to him, but he kept telling her he would call her back and never did.

Danielle took care of her kids by herself, so she was used to deadbeats, but Mike was a whole different breed, and he was the oldest out of her two other baby daddies. He just didn't seem to give a fuck. He was such a nice guy; he made her laugh and she enjoyed his company and now it seemed as if he was the devil in disguise.

A week later at a doctor's appointment, Danielle saw the baby on the ultrasound. She was nervous that she was about to have baby number three, but she knew it would be alright. The doctor wanted to do more but the computers were down, so they had her make another appointment for the following week.

The following week Danielle returned to the doctor; she couldn't wait to hear the baby's heartbeat. Once she was in the room, she was chatting with Melanie, the medical assistant, who she was cool with, then the doctor came in ready to do the ultrasound. Danielle laid back on the table as he applied the cold gel to her stomach. He moved the probe around, then Danielle saw him making weird faces. She continued to look at him and his facial expressions continued to worry her.

"Is there a problem, because the face you're making is bothering me?" Danielle blurted out.

"Well, it looks like you're not having one baby, but rather two," he said, as he turned the screen around for her to see.

"What do you mean? When I was here last week, you saw, and I saw one baby. Where did this other baby come from?"

Danielle started crying.

"He already has twins, now he gave me twins," she said with tears running down her face.

"The baby could have been hiding behind the other last week, but let me do a vaginal ultrasound, to verify what kind of twins you are carrying."

The doctor stuck a blue and white stick that reminded her of a dildo inside of her.

"Ms. Lee, I only see one placenta, so it looks like your carrying Mono Di twins, which are identical twins and that has nothing to do with him. Identical twins happen on their own. He just happens to have had two women that produced twins for him; he must be a lucky man."

Danielle rolled her eyes. That fool didn't understand how blessed he was, because he was treating his blessing like garbage.

"One more thing, Mono Di pregnancy is a high-risk pregnancy, and we don't handle those, so you can either go to Colombia Presbyterian in New York City, or St. Joseph's hospital in Paterson."

Danielle was not having her babies at St. Joseph's.

"I will be going to Columbia," she responded.

"I will have the receptionist give you the information so you can schedule an appointment over there. Take care and we will see you after you give birth."

Danielle checked out and got the information she needed to make the appointment with the new doctor she would be seeing. She was still in shock that she was having two babies. She couldn't believe it.

After finding out she was having twins, Danielle called Mike again. This time she got sent to voicemail.

Weeks turned into months and she never heard from Mike; she only heard the rumors going around about her. Mike was telling people he didn't know her and she was just pinning the babies on him because he had money and the babies were probably Stefan's.

At this point, Danielle wished Stefan could have been the father, but she hadn't slept with him in so long there was no way he was. Danielle just thought how dumb someone could have been to even think she would have nailed Stefan's baby on Mike. Yeah, Mike had street money, but every sensible person knows street money is short money. Stefan owned real assets, had a job, a 401k and life insurance—all the things a grown man should. However, it was the local females who believed that stupidity. The ones that use men for money and think a Gucci bag is an accomplishment in life because they themselves didn't come from real money, so they were the ones feeding into the rumors. Then people had seen the two around town often in the short period they were messing around so of course those people figured out right away that Danielle was pregnant by Mike when they saw her.

Danielle then heard Mike was dating an old fling he use to deal with. She wasn't from Bergen County but wanted to be down and fit in with everyone from there. Her name was Blake. Danielle looked her up on Facebook, she was about five-eight, 165 pounds, brown skinned, had a nice figure and a weave that hovered over her left eye. Danielle sent Toya a picture of Blake.

This is the chick he dissed me for, Danielle texted.

"Damn, you and her look similar," Toya responded.

Danielle rolled her eyes on the other end of the phone. All Danielle knew was Blake either didn't know about her and the babies or was just a selfish bitch and didn't care if he didn't take care of them. That right there was enough to want Danielle to break her neck.

Months flew by and Mike not once cared to call or anything.

170

Danielle felt as if the Mike she once knew was dead, and the evil bastard he was now was someone she would have never gave her time and energy to.

At three months she found out the babies were girls and at six months Danielle found out that Baby B, who she was going to name Raine had a heart defect and would need surgery after being delivered. Here she was pregnant with twins and one had a health problem and she had to walk around with her head up and not let Mike's lies and negativity make her crumble. She had to stay strong.

In the meantime, Naja was growing great resentment toward her mother. She was still feeling neglected after Danielle had Mason, and here her mom was pregnant again by another piece of shit that left her, which in turn meant Naja would have to be her helper in taking care of two more kids. Naja was even mad at herself because she had thought Mike was a good guy. He treated her better than those dumb asses Hector and Stefan, whom she had seen her mom cry over in the past. *Why does she keep picking these lames?* Naja thought.

Danielle had planned her own baby shower for April 22. She had done everything by herself and started to stress over that. She had wished Bianca had helped her coordinate it more, but Danielle was tired of asking people she thought cared about her for anything.

The night before the baby shower, Danielle received a call from an old friend that said they saw Naja walking down Teaneck Road with a boy. Naja had told her mother she was at the recreation center for the teen Friday night party.

Danielle hopped in her car with her son who was in his

pajamas and drove to the recreation center. Danielle went inside and asked the adults that were supervising if they had seen Naja. They said the name didn't sound familiar, but they said some kids had just left.

Danielle then drove up the street to Teaneck Road and spotted Naja and the boy, who was about five-five and had the brown skin tone of Mexican descent, walking together near Walgreens. Danielle slammed on her brakes and hopped out the car.

"Your ass is supposed to be at the recreation center. Where the fuck are you going and why the hell are you with him?"

Danielle realized Naja was with Dario, a boy she had already told Naja to stay away from.

Dario was trying to get Naja to be a member of the local Blood gang and after Danielle realized and put a stop to that, Dario had plotted with Naja to set Danielle up and scare her with a gun because Naja felt Danielle was too strict as a mother. The police had gotten involved when one of Naja's classmates overheard the two discussing it and told the school principal.

"Get your ass in the car right now!" Danielle screamed.

Naja had no words and just opened the passenger side door of the car.

"You little fucker. I told your ass to stay away from my daughter. If I see you with her again, I will kill your little ass, do you hear me!" Danielle yelled, as she followed Dario who was walking away. "You ugly foreign motherfucker. I'm sick of your ass!"

Danielle then returned to her car.

"We are going to Paterson. I'm dropping your ass off with Vargas. Let him deal with this bullshit, I'm tired."

"No, I don't want to go with him," Naja said, as tears were rolling down her cheeks.

"I don't give a fuck what you want!" Danielle shouted, as she drove toward Route Four West heading to Paterson.

Danielle arrived outside of Ace's new baby mother's house on Mercer Street, where Vargas was staying.

"Go ring the doorbell and see if he is inside," Danielle told Naja.

"I don't want to go," Naja cried.

"That's not my problem. Get the fuck out of my car."

Few seconds passed and Naja still sat in the car.

"Did you hear me? Get the fuck out of my car," Danielle repeated.

"Okay, I'm going, but please don't leave me here."

"I won't, you need to go talk to him. I sent him a text about what just happened. He hasn't responded, but when you go inside tell him to check his phone, I'll be out here waiting."

Naja opened the door slowly and finally got out and walked to the door. After someone buzzed her into the apartment, Danielle sped off.

Danielle was over Naja and her recent behavior. *Let Vargas take some responsibility for a change.* Danielle thought as she headed to Route Four East.

Ten minutes later, Danielle received a call from Ace's baby mom Chanel.

"Yo, what the fuck? Why did you just drop Naja off and leave?"

"Her dad stays there right? So obviously, I'm dropping her off to him."

"This is my house, not his. That is some real disrespectful

shit. Plus, he is moving out tomorrow, so you need to come get her.

"You sound dumb as hell. How is it disrespectful of me to drop my daughter off to where her dad lives? And if he is moving tomorrow, she can move right along with him, dummy."

"Who the fu…"

Danielle hung up on Chanel before she could finish what she had to say.

Twenty minutes later after arriving home, Danielle had multiple texts from Vargas to come pick up Naja because he had to go to work. Danielle ignored them all. Danielle laid Mason down to sleep in her bed and she slept until the next morning.

After waking up, Danielle had a long day ahead. She had her baby shower that evening and she had to set up and run errands. However, despite being mad at Naja, Danielle was worried about her over at Chanel's house. Vargas and Chanel acted as if they didn't want Naja there. Danielle picked up the phone and called Chanel.

"What the fuck do you want?" Chanel answered.

"Where is my daughter?'

"Where you left her at, you stupid bitch."

"First of all, I'm not going to allow you to call me a bitch but so many times."

"I don't give a fuck. Who leaves their daughter without money, food or clothes at someone's door?"

"Are you really that dumb? If her father lives there, he needs to supply those things. The way you sound, you act like you're fucking him too."

"Bitch, shut the fuck up. I will fuck you up. I don't care if

174

you're pregnant because your face isn't pregnant. Bring your ass over here."

"I'm on my way to get my daughter, so be outside," Danielle replied, as she hung up the phone.

Danielle went to go pick up her cousin Annette and her two kids from Newark. After picking them up, Danielle explained the whole situation to Annette as they headed to Paterson so Danielle could handle the situation.

I'm on my way, be outside bitch, Danielle texted Chanel.

Danielle pulled up in front of Chanel's apartment. A small crowd had formed, like they were ready to watch a fight.

Danielle pulled up in front of Chanel's house and hopped out the car and shouted, "I'm outside, where you at?"

Danielle saw Chanel running down the stairs. Soon as Chanel got close, Danielle swung and hit her. Chanel hit Danielle back and when Chanel tried to swing on her again, Danielle grabbed her by her hair and did her signature headlock move on that ass. When Danielle did that, Naja tried to hit her too. Danielle couldn't believe it. Here she was eight months pregnant with twins, fighting this dumb bitch and her own daughter was trying to swing on her too.

A few seconds later, a girl and guy came up and broke the fight up.

"Y'all can't be fighting, you're pregnant," the girl said.

"I don't care. This bitch was running her mouth like I wasn't going to pop that ass because I was pregnant."

"Vargas gave me permission to call the cops on you for child abandonment."

"Call the police then!" Danielle shouted. "Naja, hop your ass in the car."

175

"I don't want to go with you!" Naja yelled.

"Naja, go with your mother," Chanel responded.

"I'mma see you again," Chanel continued.

After Naja hopped in the car, Danielle went to go pull off, but she felt a contraction and when she pressed the gas, she ran into Chanel's parked car which she had parked behind. Danielle pressed the brake and then when she went to press the gas again to pull off, she hit the car again.

"I'm calling the fucking police, you crazy ass bitch, You're going to have them babies in jail!" Chanel shouted.

Danielle really couldn't fathom how dumb Chanel was, because Chanel would've been the one going to jail for fighting a pregnant woman, and Annette was Danielle's witness who heard Chanel say she didn't care if Danielle was pregnant because her face wasn't.

After trying again, Danielle drove off and headed to her place.

"Yo, cuz, you shot the fuck out," Annette said. Annette was standing next to Danielle throughout the fight to make sure Chanel didn't hit Danielle in the stomach or anybody jumped her in as per Danielle's request.

"Nah, that bitch thought I was just going to let her threaten me. No, honey, I am not the one and Naja, we going to have a long talk. I can't believe you really sided with that bitch and hit me! Those people don't give a fuck about you and you turn on your own mother? They didn't even want you there."

Naja didn't say anything as she sat in the back seat gazing out of the window. Deep down, she was hurt and mad. She was hurt because she knew her actions had caused all of this and she was mad because her father acted as if she was a stranger and

176

didn't want to be bothered with her or any of her issues.

"Anyway, we got to go get ready for this baby shower tonight and front like none of this happened," Danielle said with a sigh.

Danielle invited around seventy-five people to her baby shower. She had Bianca's mom make custom invites. Despite there being forty RSVPs, only about twenty people showed up. Danielle paid for everything herself and set up everything alone besides her cousin's girlfriend, Velma, coming to help coordinate some customized items she made upon Danielle's request.

Danielle's best friend, who she knew had went out of her way to help others at their baby shower, was nowhere to be found. The baby shower started at 5 PM and Danielle was at the hall setting up until five; as people showed up, she had to leave to go get dressed.

As Danielle was heading out, Bianca showed up. For some reason Danielle pictured her best friend being late or not being able to help her because she was making a dish or getting her one of the bigger gifts she had needed.

"I just finished setting up. I got to go home and get dressed."

"My bad sis, I had to work. My mom had made rice, but I didn't have time to pick it up, but I'll head back to your place with you to help you get dressed," Bianca said, sensing a bit of disappointment coming from Danielle.

"By the way, here is your gift." Bianca handed Danielle a cute little bag. Danielle opened it up. Inside were two little bracelets with a red and black chain and gold plate with each baby's name embedded in it. Danielle was thankful but assumed that best friends were supposed to come with the most needed gifts and the biggest. Danielle would've been happier with boxes of diapers and wipes that she had witnessed Bianca go above and beyond for others. She started to realize this wasn't the best friend situation she always wanted. After getting ready, the two returned to the baby shower where everyone was looking for Danielle. Danielle had spent her hard-earned money and made the best of the evening despite the day's occurrences.

Chapter 14

It was now June 2017 and Danielle was scheduled for a C-section on June 26th. Her last day of work was the 16th, so that gave her ten days to enjoy her last days as a mother of two kids.

Danielle had her last weekly doctor's appointment on the 20th. She had forgotten her phone at home but didn't think much of it because she would return home within two hours.

When she entered the room for her ultrasound, the tech did the regular routine; placed the gel on Danielle's stomach and probed around on top of her stomach. After about twenty minutes, the tech left the room and was gone for about thirty minutes. Danielle thought that was weird, but she was just ready to go home.

Finally, the tech returned with a doctor.

"Ms. Lee, it seems there is an issue with Baby B, and we are going to admit you to the hospital and have you get ready for delivery."

Danielle was not prepared. She didn't have her hospital bag, which she had already packed the previous day, and she didn't have her phone.

"Can I go home and get my phone and bag?" Danielle asked the doctor.

"We don't recommend that at all. We want you to go register on the 10th floor and have you admitted immediately."

Danielle couldn't believe this was happening. She called her phone hoping Naja would answer. After the third ring, Naja picked up.

"Naja, its Mommy."

"Hey Mom, what time are you getting back? I wanted to know if I could go to the park."

"Naja, they are keeping me. I'm having some complications and I need to deliver the babies."

"Ahh, okay Mom."

"Please clean up the house and keep and eye on Mason and don't have anyone in my house while I'm gone. Call this number if you need anything, I love you."

"I love you too," Naja said, as she hung up.

After the nurses started Danielle on the Pitocin, two other nurses entered the room.

"Ms. Lee, we got a phone call for you, about a situation at your home."

"Excuse me?" Danielle answered.

"The Teaneck police department called here looking for you. We told them you were being prepped for delivery and would relay a message. They told us that your son was left unoccupied and ended up outside crying for you. Someone called the police, so your son and your daughter are at the police department and they need you to call them back as soon as possible."

Danielle was in disbelief; she had left her sixteen-year-old daughter in charge. *How the hell was Mason left unattended?* she thought. *What if he got kidnapped, or hit by a car?* Danielle got more and more upset the more she thought about it. She wanted to punch Naja in the face, because if anything would have happened to Mason, she would've beat the fuck out of her. Danielle was so upset she no longer felt any of the contractions she was having.

After the nurses started her on Pitocin, she asked if she could use the phone to call the police department.

"Teaneck Police Department, Detective Kane speaking, how can I help you?"

"This is Danielle Lee; I received a message that something happened involving my son."

"Oh yes, Ms. Lee. We were called to your residence because your son was outside crying and calling for you. We arrived and saw your front door open and entered your residence and nobody else was there. We called your cell phone because we had your number on file from a previous incident that involved your daughter. When we called your number, Naja answered and told us she was walking toward your home, however I told her to come here immediately. When she arrived, she gave us different stories, but the timeline wasn't matching up. Finally, she admitted she left Mason alone while he was sleeping and walked to a friend's house in another town which was a forty-five-minute walk away."

"What? OMG, I can't believe this. Why would she do that?

She knows better than to leave my son alone. She is old enough to watch him. I did nothing wrong. My kids can't be taken away."

"Well, Ms. Lee, we have a DYFS worker here and she needs someone to come pick up your kids before she has to put them in the system. We suggest you give us some names and we will go through your phone and call them and see if they can pick up the kids. By the way, no you did nothing wrong, but because of your daughter's actions, we cannot allow her to return home alone with your son."

Danielle was hurt, angry, and upset.

"Can I speak to Naja please?" Danielle asked Detective Kane.

"Hold on," he answered.

"Hello," Naja said on the other end of the phone.

"Why the fuck did you leave my son home alone? Are you stupid?" Danielle yelled through the phone to Naja. Danielle had called her phone before she got admitted and Naja answered.

"You knew I was in the hospital and had to stay and you go and do something like this? If anything would've happened to my son, I would have fucked your dumb ass up," Danielle continued. "What do you have to say for yourself?"

There was a silence

"Hello, I know you fucking hear me!" Danielle screamed.

"I'm sorry, I didn't think he would wake up so soon, I just wanted to go hang with my friends," Naja answered.

"Well, if you were fucking smart, your ass would have put him in the stroller and taken him with you. You get on my damn nerves. Give the phone back to the officer, I don't even want to talk to your stupid ass anymore."

Danielle knew what she was saying to Naja wasn't the nicest of things, but Danielle kept thinking about how scared her son must've felt. How she would've felt if something would have happened to him.

"Ms. Lee, is there anyone in particular you want us to call to come stay with the children?"

"You can call my mom; she will come get them. It may take a few hours to get up here though because she is in North Carolina. She is listed in my contacts as Mom."

"We will call her right away. Hope you have a safe delivery, and we will be in touch," he said before hanging up.

After an hour, Danielle called the detective back to follow up

"Ms. Lee, your mom is on her way. The DYFS worker that is here is named Lizette. She will take the kids back to your home and wait for your mom to get here."

Danielle was relieved her mom was coming to get the kids. She was still pissed off but at least she knew her kids would be safe and sound while she delivered her twins.

"Thank you, Detective Kane," Danielle responded.

After hanging up Danielle took a big sigh of relief.

Now it was time for her to try and relax before greeting her new babies.

After a long night, the twins were finally born the next day. Danielle had a C-section; she didn't want anyone with her since she went through the whole pregnancy by herself. She wanted to end it by herself. Danielle was still upset about what was going on back home, but right now she had to focus on the two lives she was about to bring into the world.

"Ms. Lee, is anyone coming to support you during the C-section?" one of the labor and delivery nurses asked.

"Nope, I'm doing it alone.

"Well, we will be your family today then. Do you want any music? We will put Pandora on for you."

"Yes, can you put the Janet Jackson station for me?"

The anesthesiologist gave Danielle her epidural.

Danielle was so nervous; she had never had a C-section and didn't want to be cut open, but she had no choice.

They had put a sheet up so Danielle didn't see them cutting up her body, which she kind of did want to see.

"Make sure y'all please put my intestines back like you found them," Danielle said jokingly, but she was really serious.

The doctor laughed. "Don't worry Ms. Lee, we are going to take care of you."

What seemed like five minutes later as Mary J Blige's "Real Love" was playing on Pandora, Baby A was out and two minutes later Baby B was taken out, but they had to rush Baby B out to the NICU because she was blue. Danielle was able to see Baby A; she was beautiful with a head full of hair.

Once they stitched her back up, they rolled Danielle into a room where the twins were being kept before heading to NICU. Danielle saw Baby B for the first time. She was so much smaller than Baby A, but Danielle was in love; Mary J Blige's song fit the situation perfectly.

Danielle named Baby A, Sparkle Marie Lee, and Baby B was Raine Sky Lee. Danielle was taken to her room; she was finally able to doze off. Danielle woke up eight hours later and called for an attendant to wheel her up to see the twins in the NICU.

Three days later Danielle was released from the hospital. She wasn't allowed to take either baby home yet. Sparkle Marie's body temperature wasn't where it needed to be, and Raine Sky was still too weak to leave the hospital due to her diagnosis of coarctation of the aorta, which caused her to have a weak femoral artery pulse that would require surgery. She was hurt but she had to do whatever she needed to so her babies could be in perfect health.

Danielle returned to an empty home. She was glad because if her daughter was there, she would probably have strangled her. She called her mom, who was equally upset with Naja.

"Colin and I had a long talk with Naja. She said she was sorry and wants us to apologize to you too on her behalf." Danielle and her stepdad Colin didn't get along well but her kids loved him. Naja had been around him since she was born.

"Well, I really don't want to talk to her right now," Danielle said. "Thank you for coming up here to get them for me. I love you, Mom."

"I love you too, how are the babies doing? What is the doctor saying about Raine?

"They are in the NICU; Raine is in an incubator and Sparkle is on a respirator. I'm going to get some rest and go to the NICU and see how they're coming along."

"Okay Baby. Make sure you get your rest and I just want to tell you one last thing, I don't want you to have any more children after this. You have to go through so much by yourself, while these no-good men you're having kids with aren't helping you do nothing."

"I know Mom, believe me, I know," Danielle said, sounding sad. "I got this though, everything will work out. I just have to put my faith back in God and pray for guidance."

"Well, rest up and I'll call you later."

With that, the two hung up.

Danielle was able to take Sparkle home after five days, but Raine had to stay longer. Every day, Danielle travelled by bus to bring Raine breast milk and spend time with her.

Danielle tried calling Mike, but there no answer. She went on his Instagram through a fake page she had made and saw he was at Donny F's All White Party in Edgewater. He had rented a party bus for him, Blake, and their friends.

My poor baby is here is NICU and he is renting party buses for this dumb bitch and their friends. How can a man walk around and party not giving a fuck about the lives of his children? Danielle thought.

After Sparkle came home Danielle decided to go after Mike for child support since he seemed to want to ignore her calls and the babies and she filed for a paternity test, so she could put an end to the rumor that he didn't know her.

A week passed and Raine was finally able to join Danielle and Sparkle at home. At first Danielle was so tired; she had no help, and she had two babies up every three hours crying for milk. The football position where she was able to feed both babies was uncomfortable for her, so she fed them one at a time. Fifteen minutes on one breast with one baby, fifteen minutes on the other breast with the other. Then she would repeat that so that each baby would feed for a total of thirty minutes. She did this every three hours for the first four months.

When the babies were two and a half months old, Naja and Mason returned home.

You could feel the tension as soon as Naja stepped in the door.

Naja went straight to her room without speaking to her mom.

"Danielle, I don't want you flipping out on Naja. She feels alone and just wants you to show her love," Danielle's mom Linda said.

"I really don't care about how she feels. She left my baby alone. Anything could've happened."

Danielle wasn't one to let go of things so easily.

Naja overheard what Danielle had said.

"I don't care about you either!" Naja yelled from her bedroom.

"I don't even want you here, you're pathetic!" Danielle yelled back.

Naja came out the room as if she was about to get in Danielle's face.

"You better sit your ass down before I knock you out," Danielle said, as Naja stepped into the living room.

"I'm tired of you and I hate you," Naja said in anger, balling up her fist.

Danielle reached out and grabbed the broomstick that was laying up against the wall next to her and went to go hit Naja with it before her mother got in the middle of it.

"Y'all have to stop. Mason is crying watching you two yell at each other like you're not even family. Danielle, I know you're upset, but Mason's okay and I came and got them. Naja was the only child for twelve years and now you have three more, showing her less and less attention. I will not leave here until you two calm down."

Danielle knew her mom was tired, she had to drive right back to North Carolina and go to work the next day. So, Danielle calmed down for her mom's sake.

"I'm upset, but I'm going to let it go," Danielle said.

Naja apologized for the whole situation, but her and Danielle's relationship was then strained.

Danielle loved Naja but because she lacked attention from her father, she kept resenting Danielle.

Danielle finally called DYFS and asked if they could help set up some family counseling. After two weeks, the two started their first session. Their therapist Nancy, was a chubby white woman in her late twenties. Danielle loved her energy from the first day she arrived and Naja liked her as well. Nancy was able to get the two to communicate and helped ease the tension that had grown between the two.

After four months, Nancy felt the growth that had been established. Danielle and Naja had grown closer and were able to be more affectionate with each other which led to them growing a closer bond. Six months into their counseling Nancy ended their sessions seeing the progress and let the two know they no longer needed her assistance.

Danielle was hurt when Raine had her heart surgery and she had to go through it alone. She wished she had Mike's moral support because at the end of the day that is all she wanted from him. Instead, he was still denying to everyone that he knew her. Danielle was trying to be strong, but deep down, Mike's lies hurt her. She thought he was one of the good ones.

Danielle had never seen Blake before, besides through some Facebook pictures. One evening while Danielle was out with one of her friends, Ericka, who was a local entrepreneur that was well-known. They happened to stop by Regina's. As Danielle headed to the patio of the restaurant she saw came face to face with Blake. Danielle couldn't believe it. Blake looked exactly how she looked in her photos except for the fact Danielle saw her floating eye. *What the fuck? This floating eye bitch is who he is choosing over his kids? Damn, that shit would irritate me, I bet he fucks her doggy style to avoid looking at that shit,* Danielle said to herself as she chuckled out loud. Danielle didn't like to be a hater, but she couldn't believe this was what Mike was parading around town and denying his kids for. The girl couldn't even see straight. Maybe that's why she was a perfect female for Mike because she couldn't see through his bullshit.

When Danielle turned to the left, she saw Mike sitting on a lounge chair. He looked like he saw a ghost when he realized it was Danielle. Danielle continued walking on the patio and sat on the other side away from the two. After five minutes passed, she saw Mike and Blake leave.

The twins were now five months old. Danielle had fallen in love all over again every time she saw them. They were so cute, despite the fact she could see Mike's features becoming more prominent.

Chapter 15

Five months after putting Mike on child support, he had yet to take the DNA test. Danielle got a DM on Facebook from Tasha. Tasha was Mike's ex-girlfriend. She and Mike had dated for four years, four years ago. Apparently, she was the girl he was with when he cheated on her with Blake.

Tasha was light skinned, five-three, had a nice figure and big butt. She was a cute girl but very outspoken. She had even put Mike on blast on Facebook when Danielle was dealing with him saying he was an "undercover brother," meaning he liked men. When she posted that Mike had it out for her and Danielle wasn't a fan of hers even though she didn't know her.

In the message, Tasha had written Danielle to call her and left her number.

What the hell does this girl want? Danielle thought to herself.

After feeding the twins and putting them down for a nap she called Tasha.

"Hello, Tasha, it's Danielle, what's up?

"Hey girl, I know we don't know each other like that, but Mike told me to call you because he wants you to take him off child support."

Mike was going with Blake but had his ex-girlfriend who just had put him on blast for being on the down low and said he couldn't stand to tell me to take him off child support. Then he goes around denying the kids but hasn't taken the DNA test. WTF type of Jerry Springer shit is this? Danielle thought.

"Well, you can tell him, I'm not. He hasn't called me, or tried to reach out or check up on his newborn babies, especially after Raine had heart surgery and I know he knew about it but wants me to take him off child support? Not happening."

"Well, he doesn't work so he can go to court and have the judge order him to pay as low as five dollars a week, when you can take him off and he will take care of the kids," Tasha replied.

"If he hasn't tried to establish any sort of communication with me now, I don't believe he will, especially if I take him off child support. I'll take my chances. Thanks for the call and take care," Danielle said, before ending the call.

Danielle couldn't believe the nerve of this guy, having his ex-girlfriend call her. Danielle picked up the phone to call Felicia. Felicia was an older female from Teaneck, who knew Mike and his family. Felicia had become someone Danielle confided in. They had stopped talking while Danielle was pregnant because Danielle had felt Felicia was two-faced. She often talked about people behind their backs one minute and the next she would be on social media putting hearts and nice comments under their picture. Felicia had explained that even though she didn't care for them she didn't want to be on their

191

level so she would give them compliments, etc. Danielle still felt that was being fake but let it go. She still had to learn that your intuition about a person is usually right.

"Hey Felicia, what's up?"

"Hey, girl, nothing much, just trying to get my real estate business up and running again."

"Well, Mike just had Tasha call me to tell me I need to take him off child support."

"Girl, she is crazy, don't pay her no mind. First, she was talking bad about him, now she is calling you for him. Girl bye. You keep doing what you're doing. I'm proud of you, you inspire me, shit. Don't let nobody come and try to make you feel bad for what you're doing, he'll come around."

"Thank you, Fee, I needed to hear that."

They continued catching up before finally hanging up.

Felicia called Danielle a few minutes later. She was bothered that Mike wasn't stepping up and asked Danielle to give her Mike's number so she could call him.

Felicia called Danielle back.

"Girl, I just spoke to him. He said if you take him off child support, he will make sure you and your household is taken care of."

Danielle already had this proposed to her by Tasha, but she needed help. She needed another car and this could be a solution for her but something in her gut telling her this wasn't a good idea, kept nagging at her. She thought maybe an apology from Mike would make her feel better. She just wanted him to step up to the plate and take care of the twins. She no longer wanted him, he was a turn off. She didn't want him even if he was the last man living, he disgusted her that much.

Danielle took a deep breath.

"I'll go take him off child support in the morning."

"Cool, I will let him know."

Felicia then hung up to call Mike.

Something about the whole thing didn't sit right with Danielle.

Mike wanted her to take him off child support, however he never attempted to reach out to her about the kids or even offer some upfront money.

The next morning Danielle went to the courthouse to drop the child support and had to pay a twenty-five-dollar fee which Mike didn't volunteer to pay. However, Danielle had put some stipulations in the paperwork. She had written that she wanted child support only dropped if Mike paid at least five thousand dollars toward what he owed.

Coincidentally that night, Mike had got arrested for the nonpayment of child support for Danielle's twins; he owed almost $17,000. As soon as Mike got arrested and word got around, Felicia was acting like she was Mike's spokesman. Danielle started to get a funny feeling about her again.

It was the weekend, so Mike had to just sit in jail until the court date that upcoming Monday.

Danielle figured the paperwork wasn't processed yet and knew she had to go to court Monday as well to let the judge know she was dropping the child support and to release him. Danielle thought Mike would have a heart, especially since she was doing him a favor out of the kindness of her heart. Monday came and Danielle went to court. She felt that this could work out and Mike would be thankful she dropped the child support and came to court to make sure he was released. However, when in court Mike sat in the court and lied when questioned by the judge. His attitude didn't change, and she started to doubt her decision to take him off child support. However, she had given her word this time around and was able to get the judge to release him. The court had ordered they return in two weeks.

Danielle loved her kids and wanted the best for them. All she wanted for them was to have their father in their lives. Her two oldest didn't have close relationships with their fathers but they communicated with them from time to time. Mike was the only one who decided to just abandon his kids then go around like a bitch ass nigga and make up lies about her to make her look like she was the bad guy when he was the devil himself. The sad part about it was that people were falling for his lies. That was what hurt Danielle the most; that people believed the bullshit.

When they returned to court, Danielle was trying to be cordial when she saw Mike in the courtroom, especially since Felicia said Mike would come around and give her an apology. However, when they got before the judge, Mike's started with the lies again saying she was stalking him at the convenience store Blake owned, he didn't know her, and she got pregnant because she wanted to use him for his money.

After Danielle heard all of that, it helped her make her final decision and when it was her turn to speak, she told the judge she no longer wanted to drop the child support order, which angered Mike more. The petition to stop the child support was terminated.

Danielle was fed up with him lying so she no longer cared about what he and Felicia wanted her to do.

After returning home Danielle took a nap. When she woke up from her nap, she saw she had a missed call from Felicia.

Oh my, what the hell does she want? Danielle said to herself.

Danielle waited another hour to call her back.

"Hey Felicia, what's up, you called?"

"Hey, how are you? How are the kids?"

"We are good."

"Anyway, what happened in court today?"

"Nothing. Mike had a nasty ass attitude, so I changed my mind about dropping the child support."

"Yo, I gave him my word that you were going to drop the child support. Now you got me out here looking stupid. He said he doesn't know you like that and vice versa and you're trying to get him for his money."

Felicia was getting loud and saying the wrong things to Danielle. She wasn't one to argue with anyone she didn't feel was worth her energy.

"First of all, you need to lower your voice…"

Felicia, started to speak over Danielle, so she hung up on her ass.

Who the fuck does this bitch think she is? First, she called his ass a fuck boy, now she is riding with him. This bitch made it seemed she was all for my kids. I am not the fucking one. Danielle said to herself before she picked up the phone and called her dad.

"Hello, Dad. You busy?"

"No, what's up Dee?"

"I had court today and the twins' father was in there lying, but he wanted me to drop the child support, so I changed my mind. I refuse to do any favors for anyone who is trying to make me look crazy."

"It's about the kids, not about whatever you two got going on. How much does he owe you?"

"$17,000."

"He needs to give you at least half of that if he wants you to take him off child support. You can't take him off without getting something out the deal. He can say whatever, it doesn't mean he is going to all of a sudden come around if he had never made an attempt to come around before."

"Well, he won't speak to me and has my number blocked; can you call this mutual friend we have named Felicia? She just called me and got loud with me because I didn't take him off child support."

"Give me the number and I will see what we can work out."

In the meantime, Danielle started to think about Stefan. She wished they could've worked out for the better. At the end of the day, he was the one she really wanted and never stopped wanting. They were still cool, but Stefan was still kind of upset and threw her having kids with Mike up in her face on occasion. While reminiscing about him, she heard the babies starting to cry and went to go check on them.

Danielle's dad called back and said Felicia seemed nice and that she was really your friend and trying to look out for you. Danielle didn't share his sentiments about her, but thought she wasn't being fair to Felicia.

"Hello?"

"Hey Felicia, my dad said he just spoke to you and I want to apologize for getting loud and hanging up you."

"Don't worry girl, your dad seems cool, but I kept my word and you had me looking crazy and I don't play that."

"Well, I just want Mike and I to work this out and I want an apology."

"I know, but anyway I got to go. Talk to you later."

Danielle thought that was weird. Felicia rushed her off the phone when usually she talks her ear off for about an hour and then she usually must make up an excuse to get her off the phone.

Danielle had a fake page on IG and decided to sign into it and look at Mike's page.

Mike's last post was about forty-five minutes ago. It read:

"People think they are hurting you, but they are really hurting themselves!"

In the comments it showed that Felicia had commented twenty minutes prior. Under his post she put the muscle arm.

Danielle knew that bitch was up to no good. Danielle now knew why Felicia had switched sides. She went from telling Danielle how proud she was of her, and how Mike wasn't shit, to know calling Mike her "BRO." Danielle knew she was fake but couldn't believe she would help put a barrier between a man and his kids. Danielle knew all those "I'm proud of you," and "you inspire me," bullshit lines Felicia told her were obviously not genuine.

Chapter 16

A year following the drama, there were still rumors going around that she was after Mike for his money. Meanwhile, she was traveling the world with and without her kids. She brought herself a S Class 550 Mercedes and had started flipping houses and investing her money into properties. Danielle couldn't figure out what money he had that she wanted so much when she had her own and was a very successful single mother of four with no financial help.

However, the only thing Danielle was missing was love. The only person that constantly stayed on her mind, thinking about the would've, could of, should of was Stefan.

She wanted to try again with Stefan but wasn't sure how he felt about her since the last they spoke, which was over a year ago when he threw the Mike situation in her face.

Danielle decided to send him a text

Hey Handsome, you came across my mind. How is everything?

Stefan replied, *Hey Beautiful, all is well.*

Danielle was delighted he said, *"hey beautiful."* She started to blush. It gave her the courage to ask him what she really wanted.

I'm glad. I wanted to ask you something. I wanted to know if we could go out as friends and grab some food and drinks.

Nah, because I will want to have sex with you.

She knew that's what she didn't want right now, so she replied, *Why? We aren't like that!*

We used to be, until...

Danielle could see Stefan was still in his feelings. Danielle then explained how she wanted to love him for life, but Mike gave her the attention she wished he had given her, and she was sorry for hurting him. She explained she wasn't mature enough for him at the time and wouldn't have been the woman he needed.

Stefan accepted her apology and asked her where she lived.

Danielle replied with her address and asked again, *"So, can we go out for drinks?"*

Stefan never answered.

Stefan was very nonchalant. He wasn't one to openly express his feelings. Stefan had gotten hurt in the past after being in a long-term relationship. After that relationship ended, he vowed he would never set himself up to get hurt again. If he and Danielle were dating and she did what she did with Mike, he would have cut her off indefinitely, but since they weren't and he was seeing other females as well he knew he could only be but so bad. He did care about Danielle, that was the only reason he decided to forgive her, but he had walls up and didn't mind fucking her from time to time again.

She grabbed her phone when it started to ring as Naja's number popped up on the screen.

"Hey my love, what's up?"

"Mom, don't forget to stop by Macy's and get my UGG slippers I pre-ordered."

"I totally forgot, thanks for reminding me," Danielle said to Naja before the two hung up.

Danielle couldn't believe she was about to be a mother to an eighteen-year-old.

Danielle and Vargas hadn't spoken in a few years, even when she did reach out to him for help with Naja he would never call or text her back. Vargas was still playing his games and went on to have two more kids by two different women.

Mason's father ended up moving to Florida where he had a mental breakdown and last she heard he was in a psych ward in a jail.

As for Mike, he and Blake were still together. Mike was a pathetic liar and Blake was just unbelievably dumb in Danielle's eyes. Karma comes around and they would eventually get theirs when the universe was ready. However, it wasn't her problem, because she finally found her happy place.

Danielle always wondered what happened to Shante and Michelle. The last she heard was Shante had two kids by this guy she was dating and to her surprise the guy was a black guy. They had brought a house and were living happily. As for Michelle, she had three kids and was living in Fort Lee, New Jersey. The two stopped speaking after Michelle accused her of stealing steak out of her fridge one evening when Danielle had come over for a visit. As for Bianca, their relationship became strained. They tried to revive it a few times but after Bianca got involved with an older female crew from Park Avenue and East Nineteenth, they became her best friends and she called them her sisters. Danielle was basically just pushed to the side and just stopped caring because Bianca didn't give their friendship the same value Danielle saw her give to others. Danielle wished the best for her, but it was time to move on.

Danielle, however, wouldn't let Stefan go his separate way.

She refused to give up so easily, but she wanted to give him time.

A few more months passed, and one night Danielle went to the supermarket which was around the corner from Stefan's house. She decided to call him to see if he would pick her up and take her home.

Danielle called and he answered. She asked him if he could pick her up because she had too many groceries to walk to the bus stop. He told her to give him five minutes and he would come.

Danielle couldn't believe it. Maybe she still had a chance with him.

Stefan pulled up in his grey Denali and Danielle hopped in. She was so nervous her hands trembled as she held onto her shopping bags. There was so much she wanted to say to him but wanted it to come out right.

"I'm surprised you picked me up. I guess you really do accept my apology and we can at least be friends now."

It was quiet for a minute before he answered.

"Actually, I'm still hurt, but I'm working on forgiving you. That's why you're in my truck right now."

"Well, again I'm sorry. You're the only one I really wanted to be with, and I love you. I just figured since I told you numerous times that I wanted to spend more time with you and you weren't answering my calls or texts, I figured you weren't interested in me like that, so I moved on."

"I had plans for you and me. But you had sex with Mike, who I'm cool with. Not only did you have unprotected sex with him, but you had not one, but two babies with him. That fucks with a man."

Danielle started to feel bad. She hurt someone she really was in love with. She wished he had communicated his feelings before this whole situation.

"You treat every nigga you with the same too, I bet."

"What? No, I don't. You're the only one I have treated the way I do. I spoiled the fuck out of you, when I am usually downgrading a man and not doing things out of my heart but because they ask, and I feel obligated."

Danielle felt highly offended by Stefan's comment. She didn't treat every guy in her life the same because they weren't on the same level as each other. Some dudes, she never gave gifts to, or respected. She often talked down to men she dated and liked being the aggressor. Some she never gave head, some she didn't even like enough to claim. However, Stefan was different, she respected him as a man, and she would never disrespect him or use him. He was different.

When Stefan got to Danielle's apartment, they continued to talk for about another hour in the car. Danielle started to get horny and so did Stefan.

"I want to fuck you," Stefan said.

Danielle was longer into having sex and hadn't had any since 2016 and now it was late 2018. However, Stefan was so irresistible to her, the words of her favorite rapper Millyz came to mind, '*Whenever I'm with you, I feel so alive again.*' *If she had met him in real life, he would've been the only person she would choose over Stefan*, Danielle thought as she laughed to herself. The two climbed into the back seat of his truck. Danielle laid down on the seat and Stefan took off his shirt and pulled down his pants. As Danielle laid on her back, she pulled down her pants and panties. Stefan inserted his dick into her. She had gotten wet as soon as she jumped in his truck, which Stefan had always loved about her pussy; it was always gushy and snug for him. Once Stefan got his dick positioned well inside of her, Danielle gripped his dick with her pussy and held it for a few seconds every time he pumped in and would release it. As they fucked in the back seat of his truck Danielle could see from the corner of her eye that the windows were fogging up and she and hoped nobody would pass by and realize what was happening inside. The velvety feel of Stefan's smooth black skin made Danielle wetter and wetter. It felt as if her body was swallowed by him. The more she gyrated on his dick the closer she came to an orgasm. Danielle started to moan and breathe heavier before she let out a wail as her body reached its ultimate peak. Once she came, she let Stefan take over until he nutted. It felt as if their bodies missed each other, and his touch, his smell and skin felt so good to her. She couldn't believe they ended up sexually involved again. However, Danielle didn't want to be a woman on the side, or a casual fuck buddy for him. After Stefan came, he gave her a peck on her lips and the two got dressed. Danielle got out the truck and Stefan helped her to her door. He gave her one last peck on the lips before she stepped inside her apartment and told her he would call her later.

After dropping her groceries on her kitchen floor, Danielle

felt as if she would melt.

She waited for Stefan to call her and he didn't. Weeks came and went, and she refused to contact him. She wasn't going to chase no man. She thought maybe they were just in the heat of the moment, and maybe he was still in his feelings about her having twins. It bothered her and she was hurt, but as more and more weeks flew by, she let it go. She wanted to get married to someone she loved and to someone who loved her just as much or more. She had valued herself so low for so long, but now she was past that. She knew what she wanted and wasn't going to settle for anything less. She stopped thinking about Stefan and continued growing her business and taking care of her kids. Her main goal was to focus on her relationship with God.

Three months had passed since her and Stefan had had their sexual encounter in his truck. Danielle's phone beeped; it was a text from Stefan

Sup?

Danielle looked at it and ignored it. She then hopped in the shower. When she got out, she saw she had a missed call from him. Danielle wasn't in the mood to talk to him. Ten minutes later she received another text from him,

Peace out,

Danielle finally responded.

That's what you called me to say? Okay then.

Yeah, just saying hi.

Thanks for reaching out to say hi, hope all is well.

Stefan responded with a thumbs up.

That was the end of their conversation.

Danielle felt as if Stefan toyed with her emotions. He kept

her confused on so many levels that she was tired. One minute he acted as if he liked her, the next minute he acted as if she wasn't shit.

Weeks passed and Stefan finally texted her. This time he wanted her to suck his dick. Danielle declined. However, from then on, the two would occasionally text each other for a month until one evening Stefan hit her up and asked her where her kids were.

The little ones are sleeping and Naja is at her boyfriend's house, Danielle replied.

I'll be over in ten minutes.

Danielle didn't believe Stefan because ever since they had started dealing with each other, which was on and off for five years now, he had a habit of standing her up. However, Danielle got ready just in case. After Danielle hopped out of the shower, she took baby oil and massaged it all over her skin. When she got to her breasts, she grabbed them and squeezed her nipples. She then glided her hands down to her pussy. She closed her eyes and imagined Stefan inside of her. Her body jerked and she had a smirk on her face as she opened her eyes. The thought of Stefan was enough to make her cum. Danielle then put on a black tank top, and her silk black robe; there was no point of putting anything extra on since Stefan would be undressing her. Danielle lit the two candles she had in the living room and put Pandora on the Luther Vandross station. As she went to go grab her a glass of wine she heard a knock at the door. Danielle smiled; happy he did come.

Stefan came in and sat on her sofa. He had a blunt in his hand and asked Danielle for a light. While the two shared the blunt, Danielle had five million things she felt she wanted to ask and say to him, but she chopped it down to about five things.

"Stefan, what's up with you, what's up with us? I want to be with you, I want to have another baby and I want it to be with you. I want to date you and eventually marry you." Danielle figured she should stop there rather than go on and on. Stefan didn't treat her like a queen, he still hadn't taken her out or done anything for her, but there was something about him that made her heart skip.

"Yo, here you go with your emotional shit, but if you must know, I do like you, but I'm the laid-back type. I don't know if I want another kid right now and I don't want to date anyone. Did that answer all your questions? I enjoyed our time together, but I like my single life." Danielle got up to get a bottle of water, but she was actually getting up to get tissue to wipe the tears that started to trickle from her eye. He just basically told her she was good enough to fuck, but that's it. Danielle knew damn well he would've dated her if she didn't have the twins. After Danielle wiped her face with a piece of paper towel she had in the kitchen, she sat back down next to Stefan and took another hit of the blunt.

"You sucking my dick or what?" Stefan asked, as he could feel her getting emotional.

Danielle was hurt but she loved him. He was her weakness and Stefan knew that he loved the way Danielle treated him and always made him feel special. He considered many times in the back of his mind of making her his woman, but she made it so easy for him to treat her anyway he wanted.

Danielle knelt down on her knees. Even in anger, she still loved him but knew the words he just said would change her relationship with hm. It reminded her of when Pedro said he said he had love for her but was not in love with her. She held his dick in one hand and starting kissing and licking his crotch and groin while massaging his balls with her fingers. She then licked his dick up and down, then when she got to the tip of his dick, she then made a tight O shape with her lips around his penis and started bobbing her head up and down his shaft, each thrust she put his dick deeper and deeper into her mouth. She kept doing that until he came, and she swallowed his cum like she always did. She enjoyed making him cum, especially since she knew she was the only one he had been with that could make him nut from a blow job.

After she got off her knees, he told her to get on top of him, so she could get hers. She loved riding him. Danielle wasn't a fan of riding dick with all her past partners, but with Stefan it was so natural. It was as if she took the anger she had toward him and released it sexually while she was riding his dick. She felt her pussy open like a blossom when she was on top of him. In the background she could hear "Baby, I'm Ready" by Gerald Levert:

"Baby it's time, for me,
To give you all the love you need.
Baby I know that you deserve the best,
And I can't keep treatin' you, like I did the rest.
Baby I'm ready, to give you all of my love, (All of my love)
Girl I'm tired of playin games,
So many girls I can't even name."

Soon as the song ended, they climaxed. Stefan loved the way she made him feel, but he would never tell her that. They both relaxed on the couch. Danielle got up and got some coconut oil and massaged his feet as she would often do after they were intimate. took twenty minutes later, Stefan took his feet off her, put his socks on, got up and gave her a peck on the cheek.

"This is over," Danielle blurted out.

"What do you mean this is over?"

"This situation! I made a mistake because I wanted your love and attention. I tried to make up for it time and time again and you treat as if I'm not shit. I'm starting to foster a sense of hate for you. I am a good person; nobody doesn't do anything for me, and I bust my ass too much for you or anyone else to treat me like I'm not a priority."

"Well fine, if that's how you feel. We are done then," Stefan said angrily and walked out.

That felt like one of the hardest things she had to do. Danielle then started crying again and cried until she fell asleep.

Stefan called Danielle and texted her the following weeks. She never answered. She was tired of him toying with her feelings.

Danielle felt like a whole new person after letting Stefan go. She had tried to do things that pleased him while forgetting about herself.

What Danielle didn't know was that Stefan was actually in love with her, but he was scared. After being played in the past by someone he loved, he vowed he wouldn't let another woman play him for a fool. However, his feelings for Danielle were different. He knew she really did love him and knew he had pushed her away and had to stop holding the Mike situation against her.

Three weeks passed with no communication from Stefan. Danielle was starting to create her homemade all-natural skin and hair products and sell them out of her home. Naja even assisted Danielle with deliveries. Danielle finally found her peace and was happy.

One Friday evening after Danielle put the kids to sleep, she sat on the couch and rolled a blunt. After taking three pulls, she sat back and closed her eyes as her mind started to relax and figure out her next business venture. There was a knock at the door.

Just as Danielle was about to get up to answer the door, the phone rang.

She decided to pick up the phone before answering the door since she wasn't expecting company.

"Hello?"

"Hey Danielle, it's Freeze," he said in a panic

"Hey, what's going on? Is everything alright?"

Freeze was upset and Danielle could hear crackling in his voice.

"There was a shooting and…" His voice crackled and became distorted. Danielle couldn't hear him as the call was breaking up. As he continued, she heard him say "…was shot."

Frantically, Danielle yelled, "What? Who?"

As Freeze cleared his voice and repeated the name, Danielle dropped the phone.

Epilogue

Two years passed since that emotional phone call. Stefan had gained enemies over the years, mostly because people where jealous of him and his lifestyle. Stefan was shot in the back and leg. Thankfully, no major organs were hit, but it took months for him to recover. Of course, the main one by his side was Danielle. She took him to all of his appointments, changed his bandages, bathed him, cooked and fed him. Stefan realized she really was the one and knew he had to do what his heart felt was right. Five months after being shot, Stefan was able to walk on his own with an aid of a cane. That summer, Danielle's fortieth birthday was approaching, and Stefan surprised her with a big birthday party at Regina's restaurant. The two arrived at Regina's for dinner. When Danielle stepped inside the restaurant, a crowd of people shouted, "Happy Birthday!" When Danielle turned to look at Stefan, he was on his knee with a ring in his hand. He had gotten her a 3 ct. tw. Moissanite Halo engagement ring in 14k white gold. Danielle couldn't believe it; all she could do was break down in tears and kiss Stefan.

They were married six months later at the Brownstone in Paterson.

The police never discovered who shot Stefan, but word on

the street was it someone who was once close to him. Danielle had an idea who it was and gave her word to Stefan that vengeance would be hers despite his constant opposition.

Thanks to Stefan investing in her beauty company, it helped her become the successful entrepreneur she now was. After all she had done for him, he knew he had to make it up to her, especially since he knew he mishandled her during their early years.

Shortly after their marriage, Danielle found out she was pregnant. Despite the fact Stefan didn't want anymore kids, he knew that having his offspring was something Danielle really wanted.

In the meantime, Danielle contacted her brother Bobby, who had been in and out of jail for the past ten years. She knew she was pregnant, but she had vowed to take care of her family, which could have been destroyed if Stefan had been seriously injured in the shooting. She would be damned if anyone fucked with the man that held her heart. After a lot of convincing, her brother got her a 9mm Luger. She plotted to carry out her plans once the baby was born.